Praise for the w
DAVID ME

"Achingly intelligent . . . With his jump-cut shifts, startling connections and breathtaking disconnections, the author stands among our most gifted younger writers. Distinctively, though, he anneals his cutting-edge irony into a compassionate anger that goes beyond the literary times. In a word he might disdain to use, it is timeless." —Richard Eder, *The New York Times*

"His highly original stories are coats that have been reversed to show their linings . . . Means's language offers an exquisitely precise and sensuous register of an often crazy American reality. Sentences gleaming with lustre are sewn throughout the stories. One will go a long way with a writer possessed of such skills." —James Wood, *London Review of Books*

"It is Means's signature talent to view the lives of his characters, and life itself, from somewhere just beyond, in a position of maximum understanding and honorable detachment: a semi-divine vantage point for the examination of hopelessly human affairs." —Jeffrey Eugenides, author of *Middlesex* and *The Virgin Suicides*

"One thing I love about the stories in *The Spot* is that I find myself in the presence of an author whose prose, like that of the greatest short story writers, shows attention to syntax and cadence—he does not, in other words, employ the I'm-just-a-regular-moron-like-you style that so many recent American writers have employed either out of ignorance, laziness, or emulation of American politicians. Means has clearly pledged allegiance to the terrified lost souls of Americans who indomitably go on, who create the tragic comedy of this country's real life, as opposed to the one in the movies, by refusing to see themselves as lost but, on the contrary, perpetually on the verge of inheriting everything, until they are pulled under at last."

—Franz Wright, author of *Walking to Martha's Vineyard*

"[*The Spot*] is dark, deep and dangerous. Here, the author's technical authority continues to astonish. He'll switch point of view midstory or examine the act of storytelling while telling a tale that you actually want to read. His most typical pieces, at once shadowy and insanely focused, feature bleak Midwestern violence: the crucifixion of a high-school boy, or the murder of a farmer by a hooker. Others bend time until it becomes as complex as the characters themselves . . . Virtuosic."

—Leigh Newman, *Time Out New York*

"A natural storyteller, Means presents 13 nuanced tales of wanderlust and transgression. Hoboes around a campfire spin elaborate yarns in two of the richest stories, offering just enough confession to keep the others' interest: 'The Blade' finds an improbable friendship between an old geezer and a young junkie, culminating in a requisite 'blade-to-the-throat' story; while 'The Junction' pursues a vagrant who begs food at a farmhouse that is strikingly similar to the home he grew up in. The American landscape is vividly sketched in these tales, traversed by the Bonnie-and-Clyde meets Charles Starkweather team of young bank robbers in 'Nebraska,' and the manipulative con man of 'Oklahoma.' Similarly, the title story details a jaunty pimp's shameless exploitation of a girl with a horrific past, culminating in a grim discovery at Niagara Falls. There's not an off note to be found in Means's prose, and he proves to be remarkably adept at locating the sublime in the unseemly."   —*Publishers Weekly* (starred review)

"Like all great practitioners of the form, Means doesn't waste a word. There isn't enough room. His awareness of that small space necessitates a density that novelists are free to ignore. And the brilliance of these tight tales is that they're somehow about that too—a story's obligation to repeatedly hold up to a reader's scrutiny. For some, that might sound too much like literary claustrophobia, but in *The Spot*, nothing falls apart and everything is right where it should be."

—Gregg LaGambina, *The Onion A.V. Club*

"The stories by Means defy categorization . . . They are dense with detail, character and theme, and they connect in some surprising ways that aren't immediately apparent . . . The stories within the stories, like the fiction of Means through which they are framed, often have an archetypical quality transcending the characters (many unnamed), as if something immutable in the human condition keeps repeating itself."

—*Kirkus Reviews* (starred review)

"What brings illumination, and lifts these stories out of the realm of grim realism, is Means's distinctive voice, revealed in intricate, unfeasibly limber sentences which switch nimbly between various viewpoints. Magisterially detached, wryly aware of the great cosmic joke being played upon the characters, it is also full of compassion."

—Adrian Turpin, *Financial Times*

"In three previous collections, Means proved himself a master of the short form, earning comparisons to O'Connor and Carver for his tight, energetic sentences. The 13 luminous stories in [*The Spot*] are just as strong . . . Darkly comic and rich in language and drama, Means's cerebral tales are astute, amusing, and companionable."

—Jonathan Fullmer, *Booklist*

"Means is a writer of real originality with a distinct, intimate way of insinuating himself into the reader's psyche. Although only one story is titled 'The Spot,' each of these stories has its own 'spot': a fissure where the 'known present and the unknowable future' touch . . . Means knows that timing is everything in a short story. Eudora Welty wrote that a good writer knows when to click the shutter. This is exactly where Means excels. First, in clicking when characters are most vulnerably exposed, and second in implicating us as voyeurs."

—Catherine Holmes, *The Post and Courier* (Charleston, SC)

"Means was put on earth to frustrate creative writing teachers and John Gardner evangelists: His characters don't change. A lot of his action happens in flashback. His violence borders on the grotesque. He can take or leave paragraphs as structural units of composition. And he rarely, if ever, allows for immersion into fiction's 'vivid and continuous dream.' Yet to read *The Spot* is to understand that these rules were made to be broken—or, in Means's case, to be pistol whipped, dragged into a quarry, shot twice in the head, and set on fire."

—Brian Beglin, *The Rumpus*

THE SPOT

THE SPOT

STORIES

David Means

Farrar, Straus and Giroux

New York

Farrar, Straus and Giroux
18 West 18th Street, New York 10011

These stories previously appeared, some in slightly different form, in the following publications: *The New Yorker* ("A River in Egypt," "The Spot," "The Knocking"), *Harper's Magazine* ("The Blade," "The Botch," "The Gulch"), *Zoetrope* ("Nebraska," "Reading Chekhov," "Facts Toward Understanding the Spontaneous Human Combustion of Errol McGee," "Oklahoma"), *McSweeney's* ("The Actor's House"), *Ecotone* ("The Junction"), and *The Rome Review* ("All Wondering").

The Library of Congress has cataloged the hardcover edition as follows:
Means, David, 1961–
    The spot : stories / David Means. — 1st ed.
      p. cm.
    ISBN: 978-0-86547-912-8 (alk. paper)
    I. Title.

PS3563.E195S66 2010
813'.54—dc22

                                              2009042213

Paperback ISBN: 978-0-86547-851-0

Designed by Jonathan D. Lippincott

www.fsgbooks.com

3 5 7 9 10 8 6 4 2

To Genève

Contents

The Knocking   3

The Blade   9

A River in Egypt   21

Nebraska   37

All Wondering   57

The Spot   61

Reading Chekhov   75

Facts Toward Understanding the Spontaneous Human
      Combustion of Errol McGee   89

The Botch   101

Oklahoma   115

The Gulch   127

The Actor's House   141

The Junction   149

THE SPOT

The Knocking

Upstairs he stops for a moment, just to let the tension build, and then he begins again, softer at first, going east to west and then east again, heading toward the Fifth Avenue side of the building, pausing to get his bearings, to look out at the view, I imagine, before heading west, pausing overhead to taunt me before going back into motion for a few minutes, setting the pace with a pendulous movement, following the delineation of the apartment walls—his the same as mine, his exactly the same—and then there is another pause, and I lean back and study the ceiling and hear, far off, the sound of knocking in his kitchen, and then eventually—maybe five minutes, maybe more—he comes back and begins persistent and steady, without the usual aggression, as if he has forgotten me, set me aside, put away his desire for vengeance, offering a reprieve from the nature of his knocking. Maybe a five-minute reprieve, more or less, because it is impossible to guess how long these silent moments might be when they open up overhead, knowing, as I wait, that the knocking will begin again; if not in the form of his tapping heel, then some other kind of knock: perhaps the sound of the hammer he uses to pound the nails (He's a big nail pounder. He'll hang pictures at all hours), or the rubbery thud of his printer at work (He's a big printer, scrolling out documents in the wee hours of the morning, at dusk and at dawn), or the thump of his mattress hitting the slats, accompanied by the wheeze of springs (the wheeze not officially a knocking, most certainly, acting as a kind of arabesque, a grace note to the mattress knocks that arrive after some easeful swaying in his bed). Other sounds, too, that might be included in the knocking family accumulate in my mind this afternoon, an entire history of loud bangs stretching back to the day I moved in two years ago—a cornucopia of various noises that included pot/pan banging, dull plaster thud, bubbling water dribble, the claw scratch titter that continued for a week, the incessant moaning, and the grief-filled swooning sound that arose intermittently and that at first had sounded human but then, over the course of a few days, had taken on a mechanistic, reproduced quality that made me certain it was a recording, a tape loop of some sort. He was that kind of knocker. He was willing to go beyond the call of duty to find a way to make a new noise and to find a way to repeat it endlessly. He was the kind of knocker who would learn a fresh technique, a way of landing his heel on the floor, of lifting his toes and letting them rattle a board, and work with a calisthenic efficiency—all bones and sinew—to transmit the sound via the uncarpeted prewar floorboards, woody, resonant oak solid enough to withstand the harder strikes. Above all, he not only took knocking seriously but went beyond that to a realm of pure belief in the idea that by being persistent over the long term and knocking only for the sake of knocking—in other words, blanking me at least temporarily out of his consciousness, and in doing so forgetting the impulse (our brief meeting last year) for starting in the first place—he could take a leap of faith and increase his level of concentration—pure rapture—and, in turn, his ability to sustain the knocking over the long run. By casting off that original impetus (our brief hall meeting, brushing by each other on that fall afternoon so long ago), he could hit the floor with his heels while I, below, heard him and knew he was doing so driven by a pure faith that went beyond retribution. (I'd tried, long ago, to return the knocks, pounding the ceiling with the broom handle, getting up on a stepladder to follow the footfalls, only to find that as the one below, I was unable to fend off the knocking; because to knock up is not the same as knocking down, and any sound that resides at the feet most certainly isn't the same thing as a sound coming down upon the head.) Theoretically, there is still debate about the nature of the knock in relation to the listener, of course, and one can easily postulate that a knock not heard is not a knock but rather a sound—pure and simple, and that to qualify as an official knock the sound must not only be heard, but it must also arrive in the ears with an annoying quality. Most certainly, there are gentle knocks, sweet knocks, but those usually fall into the category of soft rappings: the late-night arrival, the lover-to-lover, message-through-the-wall (often adulterous) tap; the old-school, salesman-at-the-door, Fuller Brush five-knuckle rap—a deep anachronism now, replaced long ago by the doorbell, of course, which, in turn, has been replaced by the phone ring. To the receiver of the knock, all theories, no matter how plausible and how sensible, are destroyed by the sound itself. Imaginative capacities gather around the knock. A hammer against a nail, sharp and persistent, goes on a beat too long, pounding and pounding over the course of an entire evening, with metronomic precision. The rounded edge of a sap—lead in leather—being slapped overhead against the floorboards, making a blunt rubbery tap with a leathery overtone. A piercingly sharp metallic tap, not too loud and not too soft,

coming out from under the casual noise of a summer afternoon—the roar of traffic on Fifth combined with high heel taps,
taxi horns, and the murmur of voices—with a hauntingly pristine quality, the sharp end of a walking stick with a tin tip. A
swishing sound stretching from one side of the head to the other
arriving one afternoon—again, many of these knockings come
late in the day when he knows, because he does know, that I'm
in my deepest state of reverie, trying to ponder—what else can
one do!—the nature of my sadness in relation to my past
actions, throwing out, silently, wordlessly, my theorems: Love is
a blank senseless vibration that, when picked up by another
soul, begins to form something that feels eternal (like our marriage) and then tapers and thins and becomes wispy, barely
audible (the final days in the house along the Hudson), and
then, finally, nothing but air unable to move anything (the deep
persistent silence of loss. Mary gone. Kids gone). One afternoon—as I was remembering how it felt to slide my hand along
Mary's hips, or the way her skin smoothed out around her belly
and grew bone hard and then softer and flat until I got to the
soft wetness—the sweeping sound began; not a knocking, but
simply the sound of a man upstairs cleaning his apartment in
the middle of a hot New York afternoon . . . a clean, easy sound
at first. Nothing to it—no knocking—until my attention was
drawn away from reverie (Mary) and I detected within the
sound a hardness, a pressing nature, and I became aware—over
the course of what seemed to be an hour—that the sound
remained just over my head, with a steadiness that went beyond
the nature of the task. There was keen deliberateness. He was
going to sweep his way through the floor, the joists and plaster.
At some point the sweet, even anachronistic, broom swish had
shifted to knock mode, not so much the actual sound—because
that was simply vibrations in the air—but rather the inherent

pacing and gestural qualities in the way the sound produced itself: the intent behind the gesture had at some point gone from the sweeping itself to the sound that the act made, so that it was clear to me below that what had started out as a normal cleaning routine had at some point, perhaps in response to my moaning and occasional shouts up at the ceiling between sweeps, shifted over to knocking. In other words, at some point his desire to sweep morphed into a desire to knock. Another example: One relatively quiet afternoon—just the dull murmur of televisions going on all sides, the occasional voice in the air shaft—my friend upstairs decided to hang a picture of some kind, or to pound a nail for some other reason (is there another reason?), and he began with the occasional tap, teasingly working the point into the plaster. It was a tidy sound with something pleasant in it. The hammer head against the nail. Force being transferred to the tapered point, easing into the plaster, finding the gap where the plaster opens into void. I listened with pleasure. Leaning back in my chair, I thought: Go on, old boy! Pound away! Get that nail in there! Don't pause too long or you'll lose your sense of the task! Get to work! Find some semblance of rhythm in the strikes. Hold the hammer low and let it swing lightly to avoid pressure on the inside of the wrist! Get into that pure state if you can and let the head fall in accordance with the demands of the nail itself! If need be, go back into those long afternoons in the house up in Westchester, when you were neatly tied up in your matrimonial vows and waiting to see what the next project might bring in the way of quietude: some afternoon, cutting into a board, or feeling your way around a broken water valve in a dark recess. Let the pounding become one with your own sense of needing to get something done, physically, to see some effort transposed from thumb to forefinger, so to speak, smoothing down freshly poured concrete with a trowel, feeling the gelatinous shift of substance. Whatever it is, I thought, or maybe even shouted, because I was prone to instructing him when necessary and might've shouted up at the ceiling; whatever it is you're doing, get it done swiftly and with smooth strokes and avoid catching yourself up in the task itself, I thought or said. Go to it, old boy! I'm sure I said. Get into it! Pound away! The age of the handy task is waning. We're in the twilight of the age of knocking, I'm sure I said. The great tradition is on the way out, I'm sure I said, I think, because he was going full bore with a terrifying, frenetic effort, pinpointing the sound with a steady, ecstatic perfection. He was the greatest of all knockers. He was a brilliant virtuosic master of the form, landing thuds in what seemed to be an intuitively perfect way. No intent, no human intent of any kind could find such a precise way to make the sound he made. He was at the top of his form. Each knock had my name on it! Each knock spoke directly to me! His was the work of a man on the edge of madness. A man who had lost just about everything, channeling all of his abilities into his knocking. He was seeking the kind of clarity you could get only by bothering another soul, down below you (never up) in his own abode, hunkering down on a hot summer afternoon on the great insular city of the Manhattoes, trying to put the pain of a lost marriage behind him (Mary!) along with fond memories of a time when the desire he felt for his wife was equally matched by her desire for him (presumably); when there had been a great exchange of love between two souls, or at least what seemed to be, and he had gone about his days, puttering, fixing things, knocking about in a much less artistic manner, trying the best he could to keep the house in shape.

The Blade

Amid the men around the fire—tramps with other tramps—
there was a young kid who reminded Ronnie of himself from
way back, the same limberness combined with sorrow, the same
combo of despair and liveliness holding out against the odds. A
kid copping amid the others as if it didn't matter that a sense
had already formed that at some point soon he'd be cast off,
thrown from a train car or simply left behind on the road when
he was too far gone to move along. He stared the kid down and
waited for him to answer somehow.

Ignore that dead weight, the man named Vanboss said,
offering a bottle. There were among the men two bottles of Old
Crow and one of a nameless cough remedy, emerald green,
syrupy and sweet. They were in a scrubby little camp not far
from an oil refinery, just outside of Toledo, and near enough to
the Maumee to hear the water flowing. A turpentine smell filled
the air, along with the pitch of creosote coming from the track
ties and something else, an ozone aftermath of a giant electric
spark. They had a little taper of a fire going, nothing much, and
they were easeful and calm with the past as far behind them as
it would go, and for a long time not much was said besides an

occasional curse, some forswearing of the past in the form of a grunt, nothing else until eventually—because it had to at some point—a banter began between the man named Vanboss and the man named Stark, the kind of talk that came after a long quiet. The man named Vanboss told a story about a car crash. Two cars, each doing about a hundred on a two-lane outside Tulsa, struck each other head-on, mashing up into a one-foot-by-one-foot block of metal, out of which there crawled an unscratched child. That led to an argument about the likelihood—or the possibility—of such an event, which in turn led to a story about a guy who had been decapitated in a farming accident, his head boxed neatly in a bale of hay, which in turn veered into some easy, casual chatter about arrest records, which in turn led to stories of knife use, of the best way to stab a man if the need came around. (Ease into the handle and let the edge do the work if the knife is sharp, the man named Vanboss said. If dull, stab fucking hard—for the startling shock of it—and then twist even harder to make up for the dullness.) At that point, the junkie kid entered off topic, telling a tale about an old Indian man on a Zuni reservation who claimed his baby daughter had been carried away in the claws of a hawk, which led to a short, tight argument about the possibility of such an event, which somehow led back to knives and a brief silence in which they considered the way blades came in and out of their travels—a blue chrome glint in the darkness of a reefer car. A fat butcher knife—wider than it was long—whirling, blade, handle, blade handle, over the top of a loaded coal hopper. And in this silence, Ronnie held his own blade story close to the vest and resisted the urge to join in, because to tell it properly he'd have to explain how he'd spent a couple of years with an old geezer named Hambone. (But he'd never confess the deep extent of that sharing. He'd hold off on the intimacies. He'd refrain from all that.) He'd have to give the requisite road detail, charting their travails like pins on a map, from Spokane (bad facilities, not enough places to squat) to Lincoln (kind people willing to go out of their way to buy you a drink), giving just enough detail to authenticate the story, so the others would have a chance to chime in, saying, I know that town, that shit-hole, or, I stay clear of that dump, with the bulls running wild in the yards, or, I know a cop in that one, a nice guy who'll cut you a break if you need it. Then he'd have to go into how the old man had gone on a drinking binge in Flagstaff, and how he had waited out the jail stint and helped him out, and then how the old man did the same in kind a few months later, when Ronnie had evened things out with his own binge in Kansas City. The men would nod with an understanding of the delicate nature of a balanced road kinship. Finally he'd get (he speculated) to that one night at the camp in Michigan and what Hambone had said about his mother.

But at that point, in order to give the complete story (he thought), he'd be forced to backtrack. In order to give sense to his blade story he'd have to expose the old man—now gone, now just so much ashes and dust—to the judgment and ridicule of these men around the fire. Then his voice would thicken and he'd say, Here's where the knife fits in, boys. You wake up in the cold night with a blade to your throat. You wake up to a half-crazed old fuck drawing a knife against your gullet while you struggle out of a dream to a vague understanding of the threat at hand. You wake to hear an old man saying, You believe what I said about my lovely mother or I'll kill you dead right here. At that point, the story would demand more. Without more, it would simply be another blade story in a world of a million.

One more old geezer/youth kinship/betrayal tale of the road. Give me your word that you believe me or I'll kill you dead right here, he thought while the men waited, their faces tentative and masklike in the firelight, each one—even the junkie kid— holding firm with the sense that he had something to say. Beyond the weeds, the Maumee slugged casually toward Lake Erie. Another blade-to-the-throat story stood at the ready, the men sensed. They caught a vibe in the static holding pattern the banter had taken, in the way that Ronnie held off on his turn to speak. They were sure he had a blade story! In turn, he sensed their expectation, the desire they had to hear everything, right down to how he had extricated himself from the blade. Because the old geezer named Hambone was now long gone.

Just a little unloved runt packed off like a parcel. Nothing much more than a sack of flesh in cloth, passed from one relative to another, riding the line from his uncle Garmady in Detroit all the way to Chicago, where he was passed to his uncle Lester, who in turn passed him over to a Division Street neighbor lady named Urma (last name lost), who later passed him back to his mother, who reluctantly—as if holding a bottle of strychnine— took him for a week or so before saying, Good riddance, get out of my sight, and shipped him off to New York. The memories of that ride combined with the others into a panorama: small towns staring back along dark verges, lit windows buried amid hills, warm and safe but unobtainable: glowing Pugh cars loaded with pig iron, radiating heat along a siding somewhere in Pennsylvania; the long straightaway tracing the rim of Lake Erie; the rattle of the wheel trucks over the tapered tongues of switches somewhere—maybe entering Manhattan on the Hudson River line, or along the complex arrays of Gary where, years later, he'd work lighting smudge pots and greasing gearboxes. O holy vestige of memories, all those trips as a kid reduced to the sensation of being next to nothing, of being little more than a sack, curled against the seat while some bored Negro porter came to attend, his voice hangdog and low, saying, You need anything, boy? While out the window the train dug east or west through the tired back ends of yards, ran along the deep culverts and over the tops of viaducts until—in memory, at least—it came to a sudden standstill along a siding in upstate New York, where out the window a field of weeds was swaying behind some old coot, some vagabond soul lost to the road, his pants hitched up with a rope, staring up with that dull perplexity—eyes oily and stale—and then giving, in response to the boy's wave, a feeble lift of the hand, just enough to put a curse on the boy's soul and to let him know that at some point an even exchange would be made and places would be traded and the boy would take his spot on the siding and look up at the warm windows of passing train cars, the faces silhouetted behind glass. He would look up to see the shades pulled down on the sleeper cars and imagine a Cary Grant type in there watching an Eva Marie Saint type undress, her dress pooling around her feet while in her panties she rises up onto her toes to tighten her beautiful calves. He would look up and imagine that kind of scene and feel bitterness at the fact that somewhere down the line—he'd never know exactly where—he became the man on the siding looking up and stopped being the little boy looking down, Hambone thought, staring across the campfire at the kid named Ronnie, who met his gaze, waited a few beats, and then said, What are you thinking on, Hambone? (The kid—eighteen, maybe nineteen—was already starting to take on a hardness, because somewhere down the line he'd been rolled. It was there in the pale green luster of the kid's eyes, a violation. He had confessed to the fact, speaking in a roundabout manner, saying: Some men took me and tied me up and offered me a choice between two things. One of those things was death, and the other was worse than death.) You're thinking on something, the kid said again.

Hambone waited a few beats and then said, Well, Ronnie, I was thinking on a trip I took as a kid on the New York Central line—what they used to call the Water Level Route—to New York. It was grand and lovely. Nothing but plush seats and a smoking car and a dining car with full service—white table-cloths and fine china—and a sleeper car, too, with a porter who came to turn down the sheets while my mother dabbed my face clean with a washcloth and read me bedtime stories, he said, and the kid waited another few beats, and then said, I've never heard about that side of your mother. Never once heard you speak of her so kindly, and then he sat back, waiting, looking through the roil of flames at the old man, who in turn looked back with his eyes tight, pressed into the wrinkled flesh, waited a beat, then a few more, before saying, You can believe what I say or not. That's up to you. My mother was a wonderful woman. She'd do anything for me, and she did. She suffered a great deal and went through the fires of hell for my sake so many times I can't count them. I have only fond memories of my mother. I'd put her at the top of any list, he said. Then he began to cough again, lurching to the side and hacking into the darkness. When the coughing subsided, he turned back and watched the kid stir the beans one last time and then tweeze the can out of the fire, working carefully with two sticks, putting it down in the dirt to cool. Then the kid leaned back and gazed up at the sky, abject and sullen, throwing itself over the campfire. It was the kind of sky—hazy with only a few stars visible—that formed itself over a dishonest old tramp. Deep in the darkness, past the sound of crickets, the railroad tracks ticked, giving off heat, or maybe—unlikely but maybe—releasing the tension of a train traveling along the fishplate joints, an unscheduled manifest out of Chicago, or farther west in the hinterlands, somewhere past the Mississippi where, months ago, Hambone had confessed the truth about his mother: A nasty cunt is what my old lady was. A real piece of work without a kind or decent bone in her body. You'll have to take my word on this, Ronnie, because it's all I can offer. If I could I'd bring her here for you and prop her up just so you could bear witness to one of the nastiest pieces of work, I would, just to prove it, but I can't because she's dead as a doornail. Thank Christ. I'm free of that burden, at least. No matter what I can say about my time in this world right now, I can at least rejoice that she's gone, he said. Then he'd launched himself into a four-day whiskey binge in Flagstaff, one of those rant-and-rave runs that landed him in jail. (Ronnie stuck around, waiting out the jail stint, sleeping beneath a local overpass, checking in on occasion with a desk sergeant named Franklin. Who is that man to you? Franklin had asked. My father, Ronnie said, evoking a steady, doleful stare from the police officer. Your father? Yes, sir. My old man.)

There are things you can and cannot say about your old lady on the road, Hambone's Flagstaff binge had stated. There are secret limits to the evocation of anger and hatred when it comes to speaking of she who bore you out of her loins. You can say what you want about the one who brought you forth into the world, but don't go so far as to call her a cunt. The basic physics went as follows: You made a confession to your fellow tramps, usually in the form of a campfire rant, words pounded out of a pent-up grief, and then you used that confession as an excuse to tear into a drinking binge that would, in turn, serve to reveal an inner torment so deep and wild that it could manifest itself only in the form of a dismal creature, a man alone, crawling along the roadside, ignored by passing cars, his knees bloody, with no love in the world.

You're a stupid fool for holding out around here for me to come out, Hambone had said, walking bowlegged out of the Flagstaff jail. The fact that you did so simply shows your foolhardy youth.

Didn't you check some gear when they took you in? Ronnie asked, holding him up and feeling the frail, chicken-bone thinness of his shoulders.

Nothing I ever want back. Some old duds, and a canteen of whiskey they poured out for my own sake.

Long days of windblown dust and cold nights beneath starlight and yet somehow they stayed together, watching over each other, taking turns, trying to maintain a balance. For his part, at a campfire near Kansas City, Ronnie confessed to having abandoned a bride back in Ohio, a girl named Rose who had been with child—knocked up, pregnant, take your pick. As beautiful as a fucking voodoo doll, he added. He went on with his confession until his voice gave way and he slipped away from the fire and stumbled off into Kansas City—all cowpoke delusion and gunslinging hee-haw!—where he found himself, in the end, after a long binge, bloodied with a broken jaw (wired shut) and a ten-day jail stint. During which time Hambone, using the incarceration as an excuse (ten days in a K.C. pen is equal to a month in a Chicago clinker), hooked up with a hayseed named Stills and went on a ten-day burglary spree. (The old lady I burgled ain't gonna miss what I took, he explained, escorting Ronnie out of jail. She was demented and hardly knew what was what. In any case we kept things even and didn't go too far and left her a pearl brooch, a pair of earrings—silver plate—and her reading glasses. We burgled the old lady and then Stills robbed me and now I have just enough to buy a few bottles and to hold a little cash on the side to give someone else out there something to rob from us if they come along and feel so compelled.)

From K.C. they wandered east again, skirting town centers while between them a tension formed. If the price were high enough, one man would rob the other if he could, if enough funds entered into the formula, Ronnie began to admit to himself. A structure had formed around this possibility of betrayal. A tightness entered the way they spoke to each other, wedged apart by the fact that even after the drinking binges, Ronnie was still youthful and the old man was still old. To go off alone would be to stretch the you-did-this-and-then-I-did-that fights they sometimes had, mostly in Indiana, a state too prim and proper and boring around the edges to exploit. In any case, the old man's health was going downhill fast. At a free clinic in Indianapolis a doctor pressed the cold cone of his stethoscope to the caved rib bones and said, Breathe deep, deeper. Is that what you call breathing deep? When he slapped the X-ray film onto the light board in his office, it showed not shadow but rather ghostly white furls of tumor, billowing like smoke. In contrast, Ronnie remained limber and quick, fast on his toes, with lean skinny arms—only a few track marks and one hook-shaped scar from a knife fight in Akron—and a brightness in his eyes that stayed on the edge of being hopeful. A spark still burned when he spoke about ideas he had on how to make a buck, heists he might pull if he could get his old buddies back together: a forlorn gas station, not far from the Ohio Turnpike, with a single attendant behind the counter, just begging to be stuck up, just asking for it when the time was right; a blueberry farm in Michigan that would yield up a month's worth of sweet eating if you felt like heading up that way.

You got something to say on blades, the man named Vanboss said that night, outside Toledo. The silence had continued to open around the men, stretching down to the shore of the river and past that to the refinery, wagging its burn-off plume into the sky. It was a wide silence that spread out in concentric circles with Ronnie at the epicenter and the men just one ring out. It was the kind of silence that formed around a given, and the given was that Ronnie had a good blade story to tell, most likely a blade/fight story, and—this was pure speculation, but they sensed it was possible—even a terminal act of violence on Ronnie's part, because he seemed the type: gaunt, tight-lipped about his past. He had uttered the name Hambone once or twice before going on to some other subject, as if testing to see who might've known the man.

Don't have nothing to say on the matter of blades, Ronnie said, studying the flames, feeling his story tighten into something sharp. One last bit of trust the old man had handed over, in the form of how he had died and at whose hand that night. It was something he'd hold as long as he could, years hence, until he forgot most of the details and was moving through a vague

sense of what had been. But for now he recalled the blade pushing harder against his throat, unwilling to budge no matter
what he said up into the darkness. (Christ, I believe you. Your
mother was one of a kind. She was wonderful.) Beneath the
blade the hollow of his windpipe waited; an airy emptiness
ready to form. A gape through which the rest of his life would
pass. An obscene hole. The blade had not lightened up. It
remained persistent and tight, sliding ever so slightly under the
old man's grip, nicking and digging until, in a single, quick
movement, he lashed up, acting as fast as he could to save himself. Then the blade went in and out, moving before thoughts
could form. It plunged between the brittle ribs and penetrated
the cloudy center while the old man gave a loud, bellowing
wheeze, tumbling back a few steps into the fire and, falling into
a bloom of sparks, unleashing the scream that would spin
around in Ronnie's eardrums forever. It was a scream that
would never leave the world, he thought, looking at the men
who had stopped waiting for him to speak and were readying
themselves—their faces taking on a bored slackness—to move
on to some other subject.

A River in Egypt

The hot air in the sweat chamber—as the nurse had called it, ushering them in—was humidified to make it even more uncomfortable, and when he loosened his tie he was reminded that he was the type who felt it necessary to dress up for hospital visits, and for air flights, not so much because he had a residual primness left over from his Midwestern upbringing, which he did, but because he felt that he might receive more attentive service if he came dressed with a certain formality, so that the nurses and doctors tending his son might see him, Cavanaugh, as a bigshot banker instead of an assistant art director who was known, if he was known at all, for his last-minute design fixes. For example, he had once turned the interior of a hotel lobby—one of the last of the classic (now defunct) SROs in midtown, the Abe Lincoln, just off Twenty-eighth and Madison—into a Victorian salon by throwing a few bolts of velvet around the windows of the downstairs smoking lobby.

Just that morning, as he was leaving for the hospital, the director, Harrison, had called to let him know that he was being dropped from *Draconian*, a big-budget sci-fi production that included a huge political convention scene, filmed in an old dirigible hangar out on Long Island—a design job that had drawn upon his expertise in plastic sheeting, banners preprinted with mock structural details, and so forth. "It's not that we don't like your work," Harrison had said. "You've got fine, visionary abilities. You see things others miss. But maybe you see too much. The problem with your design was—and I don't know how to put this—it was too real, too clear. You know where I'm coming from? One wrong move cinematographically and you're lost in the future, or lodged too far in the past. We made one wrong move, and I don't want to make another. I'm not casting blame. I'm apportioning fault. If I don't do it, the audience will. You see, my hope is to keep the film, for all its futuristic overtones, closely rooted in the present moment, and that way, as I see it, the audience will feel connected to *contemporary experience* in a way that will allow the obvious *eternal* elements"—Harrison was apparently referring to the assassination attempt, and to the corrupt, smooth-talking monomaniacal presidential candidate who was secretly implanting electronic doohickeys into his opponents' temples in order to create a network of paranoid, deranged sap-souls, as he put it—"to resonate fully not only with current audiences but also with future audiences. So the trick to fostering believability lies in tweaking the extremely fine fissure between the known present and the unknowable future. If it's tweaked correctly, even years from now an audience will ignore the errors and focus only on the viable world that had once really existed, and still exists, in all human interaction."

Cavanaugh pondered all of the above—along with images from the drive that morning over the Tappan Zee Bridge and the beauty the river had held, stretching toward Tarrytown, rippled with tight wavelets, shimmering blue under a pristine sky—as he held his son, Gunner, in the sweat chamber, talked to him, got him settled, and gave him his toys, extracting them one at a time from an old green rucksack. These toys had been put aside for a few days so that they might accrue some elemental new-ness again and, in turn, give more in the way of pleasure. ("There are enough old toys to keep him busy," Sharon had insisted. "I can't charge another toy on the card, and I think we should build up his desire so that when Christmas comes there's not another huge letdown like there was last year. Case in point: You bought him that Gobberblaster gun last summer, which was totally inappropriate for a kid his age and might've been a perfect gift for Christmas a couple of years from now, and he went out and shot it a few times, and now it's in the back of the closet like all his other junked toys.")

That fight about buying Gunner some new toys for the test, he thought, dabbing the sweat from his brow onto his cuff, had really been spurred on by the fact that Sharon was now back in practice, commuting into the city to scrounge clients and taking on a disproportionate number of pro bono cases, as if to keep the financial burden firmly on his side of the ledger, because she felt—and he knew this from their ten years together—that pres-sure was good for him artistically, and that he'd find the strength to break through to the big time only if he pushed against the weight of their monetary need. So he extracted one toy at a time and watched as Gunner went to the floor, tinkered and fussed and depleted each quickly, and in less than ten minutes had already gone through the Emergency Tow Truck and something called the Question Cube after two lame questions:

What river is in Egypt? the Nile? the Hudson? the Thames? or the Kalamazoo?

And then:

Who said: Sometimes a cigar is just a cigar? Groucho Marx? William Shakespeare? Sigmund Freud? or King Edward?

before the Question Cube gave a weak static snort and faded into silence, so that little Gunner, who was really too young to know the correct answers, but who liked the sound of the toy's artificial voice—a basso profundo—and got a thrill out of guessing, stood up and, with a grunt, gave it a hard kick. Then he went on to quickly sap the Zinger, a gravity-defying top that was said to have the ability—in correct conditions—to spin eternally, and his old favorite, Mad Hamlet, a strangely compelling action figure that went into suicidal fits when you pushed a button hidden on its back. Only ten minutes in the sweat chamber had gone by, and all Cavanaugh could do was wait a few beats while Gunner looked up, bright with anticipation, and then cried, "I'm hot, I'm hot, I'm hot, hot, hot."

At this point, stalling for time, Cavanaugh put the rucksack out of sight behind his back and waited a few more beats before pulling it out again, saying, "Hey, hey, look, another rucksack," and shook it near the boy's head until he stopped flailing around, looked up with his ruddy face (the kid had what the doctor called dermagraphic skin—highly sensitive, prone to rashes), and said, "Give me, give me." At which point Cavanaugh unzipped the rucksack slowly and said, "Let's pretend it's Christmas morning and we're just up, having had our

traditional morning cocoa and sweet roll"—Christmas was the
one morning each year that they opened up the tightly packed
dough, popping it against the counter and rolling out the spiral
of cardboard foil—"and now Santa's bringing some new presents," and then, with great flourish, saying, "Ta da," he reached
in and pulled out the Emergency Tow Truck again, squat and
malformed, with a thick front bumper, holding it out and
watching as Gunner's face composed itself around a cry, re-
strained itself for a second, his tiny mouth a tight rictus of pink
next to which his cheeks bunched to reveal a remnant of his
original baby face—womb wet with sweat, blue with blood, and
dramatically horrific. Cavanaugh searched the boy's face the
way a sailor might read the twilight sky, and saw clearly that he
was about to unfurl a squall-cry, a true record breaker on the
scream scale. And he did. When it came, it was a squawking,
ducklike sound, odd in its guttural overtones, yet paradoxically
bright, shiny, and thin, like a drawn thread of hot glass. This
was a cry that said: You led me to believe, fully and completely,
that I was about to receive a newborn toy, something that would
match my deepest expectations. This was a cry that rent open
the universe and, in doing so, peeled back and exposed some
soft, vulnerable tissue in Cavanaugh's brain.

So that what he did next was, he thought later, simply an act of
self-protection, reaching out and yanking the boy onto his feet
and into one arm and then, with the cup of his hand, sealing the
kid's mouth shut, so that all Cavanaugh felt was the small, frail
puffs against his palm as he spoke down into the hot, sweaty
bloom of struggling face, saying, "Jesus Christ, Daddy was just
playing a game, a Christmas game. Daddy was just trying to

lighten the situation and keep you from doing what you're doing right now. Daddy just wants his Gunner to behave himself, if not for the sake of the nurses—who, I'm sure, are out in the hall about to bust in here to see what's going on—then for Daddy himself, who is at his wits' end and wants this test to go as smoothly as possible." At which point, as if on cue, the door opened, bringing in fresh air that smelled of disinfectant and hospital floor polish, and a nurse, beautiful in her tight uniform, with long blond hair, who said, "Oh, dear," and presented a face, he later thought, that was readable in an infinite number of ways—soft around the mouth, with a wry smile that just about verged on a frown, set in a snowy Nordic topography of bone structure. From the nose down, she seemed to be frank and nonjudgmental, her mouth loose around unavailable words; from the nose up, her two intensely blue eyes and a single raised eyebrow seemed to be saying: Something funny's going on here. Something's not right. Something's deeply wrong about the way you're cupping the boy's mouth in relation to the way he (the boy) is standing, in relation to the way you are looming behind him, in relation to the sheen of his terrified face, in relation to that cry I heard out in the hallway, which was so loud and shrill it penetrated the door and reached my ears. And then she tilted her face slightly to one side, glanced at the room (really nothing but two chairs and a heating unit lit with stark neon), and made a face that seemed to admit: Maybe for you, as a father, this is a trying test, though it's certainly nothing compared with a bone-marrow biopsy, a spinal tap, or the claustrophobia of the MRI ring. But, yes (her face seemed to say), the analysis of the sweat in order to rule out, or to rule in, cystic fibrosis makes it oracular in nature, and in a few hours you, sir, will be offered up the results, and said results might give you a positive yes on the disease, which would mean, of course, that Gunner will face a future of hard breathing, clotted phlegm, and, most certainly, a relatively early death (in his thirties, if you're lucky), but all this in no way excuses you, sir, from what appeared to be transpiring when I passed the door and heard the cries and stepped in to take a look.

In response to what he seemed to be seeing in her facial expressions, Cavanaugh said, "We're fine, just a little misunderstanding about the toy bag, the rucksack here, regarding Christmas, pretending it's Christmas, trying to keep him calm. I mean to say," he said, as he fingered the dimple on his tie, "I was trying to recharge these toys, so to speak, to make them surprising again, you know, and Gunner became disappointed and began to cry. Not that crying isn't normal in these circumstances."

Something stony seemed to enter the nurse's features as she listened, taking another step into the room, nodding slightly, looking down at the boy and then up at Cavanaugh. Did her eyes narrow slightly? Was there a shift, barely perceptible, in the set of her teeth? Did some interrogative element enter her eyes, brightening the corneas? It seemed to him that she was thinking: We clearly have a situation here. To cup a boy's mouth like that is wrong, sinful, actually, and just a precursor to more violent acts; God knows what's going on behind closed doors. And it seemed to him that her face (and the way she moved up to Gunner and touched his head lightly, patting him, and then moved to adjust the collecting device) also said: I've seen a thousand such moments, entering rooms to witness patients adjusting their postures, ashamed, awkward around the impersonal equipment, awaiting test results that may change their future. I've entered rooms to find patients yanking out IV needles. I've opened the door to scenes of fornication, to urine-stained old

men with pocked behinds. I've opened doors to couples en-
folded in weeping embraces, so seized with grief that they
had to be pried apart. I've opened doors to bald-headed chil-
dren with angelic eyes and shattering smiles. But this is different
because of the cry itself—the desperation and the tonal quality
in relation (again) to your unusually guilty face, in relation
(once again) to the boy's self-protective, conspiratorial slack
expression, as if he were hiding something, in relation (once
again) to the position of the hand held over the mouth, in relation to the finger marks on the flesh around the mouth. Then
her lips tightened and her cheekbones—yes, cheekbones!—
seemed to sharpen, and her face seemed to say to Cavanaugh: I
might have to report this to the resident social worker, just as a
matter of protocol. Not because I'm absolutely certain that you
struck the child but because I'm *not certain*, and if I don't do it
and further harm comes to this boy I'll never forgive myself and
I'll sit forever down in my own particular hell.

Then the nurse said, "Oh, you poor little boy. We're a long way
off from Christmas. But we're not a long way off from finishing
the test. You're a brave boy. A brave, brave boy."

Woe to the man whose child is on the verge of a diagnosis, her
face then seemed to say as she ran her fingers along the tape,
removed the electrode wires, cleaned Gunner's arm with a gauze
pad, secured the collecting device, checked the tubing, and then,
without another word, heaved out of the chamber, latched the
door, tested the seal, and glanced back through the oval window
with a face that said: I understand that your game with the toys

in the bag was creative and a sign that you're a good father, if somewhat desperate, and then she was gone and he turned to Gunner and said, "Daddy got in trouble because you were crying. Daddy got scolded, not verbally, but facially, so let's pretend again, and do the Christmas grab bag, but do it right this time and really pretend I'm Santa." And he opened the bag and pulled out his trump card, a toy he had left out in the first rotation, one of Gunner's all-time favorites, Weird Willy the Spasmodic Doll. When switched on, Weird Willy flexed and yawed spastically, like an injured athlete, and performed a ballet of crude movements while his internal mechanisms poked and prodded through his rubbery skin. The toy, seemingly crucified from within, proved agonizing to watch. Not long ago, back in August, Weird Willy had provided a full afternoon of entertainment in a patch of sunlight beneath the dining room table. Gunner and Willy had spent a good hour conversing, Gunner saying softly, "Stop that, you stupid freak, you pathetic idiot, you stupid stupid." Now, in the sweat chamber, Weird Willy said, "Haa wee, haa wee," while Gunner said, "Die, die, die," and wrung Willy's torso with both hands, trying his best to tear him limb from limb.

"And that was the end of Weird Willy, the end of the toys, and the end of my Christmas morning scheme, as I think of it now," Cavanaugh muttered to himself as he started home from the hospital, barely moving his lips over the words, imagining what he might say to his shrink, Dr. Brackett, at his next appointment. In the rearview mirror, Gunner, strapped into his safety seat, gave him a suspicious frown. Cavanaugh closed his lips and imagined saying, "When I'm with him, I'm always aware of

the value timewise. I mean, in terms of using up time, of entertainment value, so to speak, of whatever catches his attention.
Even when I'm not with him. For example, just a few months
ago I was on location in California, working on *Draconian*, and
I was driving up the Pacific Coast Highway, trying to solve a
design problem. President Gleason, after his big defeat, goes off
on his own for a few weeks to a cabin near Big Sur to ponder his
past and begin writing his memoirs, because he sees himself—
according to the script—as part of a great lineage of memoir
writers stretching back to Ulysses S. Grant and, strangely, up to
Jack Kerouac.

"Anyway, I envisioned the scene as a biblical moment that
mirrored Jesus' desert solitude. Something had to point away
from the stereotypical writer gestures (Gleason leaning mo-
rosely over his laptop keyboard; Gleason flipping his pencil
between his fingers, biting his lip, pacing the room; Gleason
pouring himself a huge glass of Scotch and swirling it gently
before he takes a drink) and direct the audience subtly to the
deeper perplexities of his crestfallen state. So I designed chinks
in the cabin's mortar that, when lit from behind, shot small
beams—or maybe you'd call them shafts—of light through the
walls and the dust motes, forming crosses through which he
might walk during one of his pacing-for-inspiration scenes.

"In any case, I was driving up the coast, thinking about this
problem, when I became acutely aware of the vista—the hard,
purging waves roiling in, the whitecaps foaming far out, and the
milky blue of the water—and it suddenly occurred to me that I
could, with great precision, calculate the exact amount of time
that Gunner would, if prompted (*Hey, Gunner, take a look at
that*), examine each scene before turning away. I could deci-
pher—is that the word?—the exact amount of entertainment

value specific scenes on the coast would offer my boy. Waves slamming around hard, bountiful rocks, breaking in a dramatic foam, no matter how fantastically beautiful, would distract him for twenty-eight seconds. Sea lions—if we walked down to get a close look—would tap out at three minutes of distraction value. A frigate, viewed through a pair of field glasses? Five minutes and thirty seconds. A supertanker, not too far from shore, but in heavy surf on the edge of trouble? Six good, solid minutes. (The field glasses would have to be new and never used before.) A frigate on fire? Seven, or possibly eight, minutes of attention. A supertanker engulfed in a raging inferno, belching a thick plume of fire? Nine. A sinking ship (with attendant oil spill and terror-stricken passengers waving frantically, some of them dashing across the deck, on fire)? Ten minutes. Albeit none of these calculations, no matter how accurate they might have felt, were really precise, because one had to go plus or minus twenty seconds on one side or the other to account for various other distractions (fiddling, scratching, eye rubbing, and snot blowing) that might cut into his attention span.

"So you see, to get to the point, when I handed him Weird Willy I had the toy figured at less than a minute. What does any of it matter, his crying, so long as he sweats enough to fill the fucking testing device, I should've thought. I should've thought, I'm lucky that my son is just crying and not spazzing out, or giving me a much harder time. I'm lucky that he's only being tested for this disease and hasn't been handed a diagnosis: terminally ill, with only a few weeks, or a day, or even less, to live, for sure, and that this is still a wide-open thing," he would tell Dr. Brackett, at his office in White Plains.

Outside, down in the street, the traffic signals would be cheeping, making a sound meant to guide the blind, if there were any. In the four years that he'd been going over the bridge to visit Dr. Brackett, he had never seen a single blind soul using the audible signals to cross the street. The streets in White Plains were always dusty and forlorn, and somehow reminded him of a Western town just before a shootout; folks were hidden away, peeking out in anticipation of violence. Even up in the office he'd feel this—while hearing the cheeping sounds—and it would form a backdrop as Dr. Brackett, a small, lean, sharp-chinned man, placed his palms on his knees and leaned forward to say something like:

"It is perfectly possible that you didn't loosen the collecting device when you grappled with your son. After all, the nurse came in and adjusted it, didn't she? You can't be blamed for that. I'm sure it happens all the time. In any case, let's focus on the wider theatrics of your parenting actions: Do you think you're the first father to cup his son around the mouth? You're a good man with a clean heart, not perfectly clean but clear (yes, a clear heart), and you had good intentions, and you were just at the end of your rope, and so you naturally felt frustrated and fearful—above all fearful, because what the test meant, most certainly, one way or another, was the central element/key/crux in the parental drama (let's call it a drama, not a play). You were fending off, or, rather, delaying for as long as possible, the end result of the test, perhaps subconsciously. You were biding your time with Gunner, trying to fend off, if I may use that phrase again, his anxiety, or what you imagined was his anxiety, by inducing play, a certain level of play, presumably, not just us-ing up time or trying to keep him calm, as you claim, but trying to keep the scene itself stable and quiet on some level, maybe thinking, as you tried, that in doing so you'd also somehow, and perhaps this is a long shot"—he would admit, because Dr. Brackett, as a shrink, liked to counter and undercut his own statements as a way of enlivening them, making them seem like organic, natural formations in order to assure his patient that he was just as human as the next guy and didn't subscribe to the old formalities of Freudian methodology—"but perhaps you were also under the belief that, somehow, if you kept Gunner quiet and calm, the outcome of the test might be positively affected. Because you believed, I believe, that there were, and are, deeper factors at play—quantum/God/mystical, take your pick—and that if the test went smoothly the results were more likely to be negative. You felt, at that moment, in the sweat chamber, after the toys gave out, a sense that in the heat of the room, and in the sweat that was being exuded from Gunner's body, fate was at hand, so to speak." (Here Brackett would draw a couple of deep breaths.) "Now that you know that the results of that particular test were inconclusive because the collection device came loose and, in the end, not enough sweat was collected, you blame yourself for the fact that you've got to go back next week and again reopen that door to the question of his health, and that in doing so you must once again face the possibility that he has cystic fibrosis, and that your life will change again," Brackett would say.

"Now let's backtrack a little. The nurse, who presumably has been through many of these moments with many other patients, most likely came into the so-called sweat chamber to offer assistance, to help you in one way or another, or to remove the electrodes, and in seeing your hand over Gunner's mouth she understood your predicament and sympathized with it and with the boy's predicament, too—perhaps your own more so than the boy's—and at that moment she did not judge you as harshly as you'd like to think, but was actually waiting for you to speak, and in hearing your anger, when you did speak, and within it your deep, almost Jobian fear, felt her own helplessness before all the illness she has faced, as you were saying. Bald cancer heads, forlorn eyes, tears, kids suffering at the deepest level. Kids cheery and chipper against the saddest odds. Kids with that disjointed misunderstanding of their own place and status, not only healthwise but otherwise, too. Kids bucking themselves up heroically. Clearly, just going by the fact that you continue to mention what her Mona Lisa face seemed to be saying, almost obsessively, it seems to me, it becomes evident that you were turning to her as a soothsayer, and maybe that might mean, and here I propose this only as a theory, a useful one—perhaps, perhaps not—that she, too, felt herself to be unwillingly put into a shamanic position; no, let's correct that and say an oracular mode. Let's say she felt that her face might—from your point of view—be seen as an oracle, and let's say that that might explain the strange expressions she presented, if they really were strange."

Cavanaugh imagined all of the above as he drove back over the Hudson while Gunner slept in the backseat with his head lolling to one side and his tiny mouth open around his own breath, and, down below, the river fretted with bits of white chop as the first hard wind of the fall drove down from the north and cut past Hook Mountain on its way to the city. As he drove, he began to cry, openly and with stifled guffaws, the way a man must cry when he is faced with the future, any future, a good one or a bad one, and after he has sat alone in a room with his child, waiting for sweat to collect so that he may know something about what is to come, some exactitude in the form of a diagnosis; he cried the way a man must cry when he's driving, keeping both hands on the wheel and his eyes wide open through the blur, and he cried the way a man must cry when he is exhausted from being up deep into the night while his boy coughs up almost unbelievable quantities of phlegm, clearly succumbing to a disease process—as his doctor called it—that at that point was indeterminate; he cried for himself as much as for his son, and for the world that was unfolding to his left, an open vista, the gaping mouth of the river, which at that moment was flowing down to the sea, hurrying itself into the heart of New York Harbor. He was crying like a man on a bridge—suspended between two sides of life, trapped in the blunt symbolism of the spans, and atop the floating pylons that sustained the decks of reinforced concrete—while his son slept soundly, unburdened now, it seemed, when Cavanaugh looked back at him in the mirror, and afloat on his own slumber. Not at all sick, or diseased, and free from whatever torment the future might offer up. By the time (three minutes later) that Cavanaugh was exiting off the thruway and driving down Main Street (six minutes later), past the stately trees unfurling their fall brilliance, he had collected himself and was clear-eyed and in a new state. He wasn't a man reborn at all. Not even close. That would come much later, after the second test, and when the results were in, conclusive and hard, no nonsense in the statement they made. That would come (he imagined) when he gave himself over to the fact that salt moved chaotically in and out of certain cells, and that Gunner's body would forever confront certain facts: mucous blockages in his lungs and pancreas, and frequent infections. But for now, as he entered the town on a beautiful fall day, the diagnosis was somewhere off in the remote future, and he was alive and dealing with the moment at hand, which included his own actions in the sweat room, and the failure of his set design for the convention scene, and he felt himself growing calm before the sweet presence in the backseat, which came to him in the form of a soft snore, a little clicking sound that accompanied each exhalation, and then, finally, a small groan as the car settled over the curb of the driveway (eight minutes later) and came to a stop, and then another slight sniff as his boy awoke (one minute later), roused by the silence, the lack of road noise, and opened his eyes and blinked, and then said, "Are we home? Are we home now, Dad?"

Nebraska

Where else to begin but beneath the dining room table, where she's hiding, dazed and alone, tormented by fear and loneliness, lost to time (it seems), most certainly to be forgotten? The annals of history won't record this lonely moment while the house cracks in the heat, aches high up in the rafters, snaps along the joists; the genuine linoleum in the kitchen glistens oily to the touch, the trees and grass sway in the wind off the river, and she hunches down beneath the table, where she at least feels safe, listening to the wind as it lifts through the trees to make a hushed sound and then depletes itself so that a dog's bark, husky and dry, can arrive from far off, and then even farther away a soft hooting sound—someone calling—and then another dog, giving a sharper, more precise bark while she examines her knees, worn to white threads, and then extends her legs and says aloud as she touches her shins and ankles, You've got good long legs, fine, fine legs. She leans back and looks at the underside of the table, the battered legs and feet (Who left this grand artifact here?), and then, looking up, sees the words GRAND RAPIDS stenciled on the underside of one of the leaves.

.

How much despair is inherent in lifeblood, to put a name to it
and yet to avoid speaking of it; they were that deep underground—and the underground was ethereal, nonexistent, and
supplanted by their own hopes. It was all vainglory. It was all
desire to overcome some inner chink in the armor—or so they
thought. Light seemed to seep through the cracks; that's how it
felt—as if they were able to read each other's minds. She could
look into Byron's face; she could see it in his eyes, his wide
brown eyes, nothing like doubt, nothing like that at all, but
some immutable glint of fear. It is fear that will destroy us, he
hinted: One wrong move and we're doomed, and so when we
approach, it must be with the utmost certainty and firm-
footedness, not a bit of room to spare, not an inch one way
or another. The line on the map indicated the route to the
mall. The Brinks truck—heavy and swaying under its armored
weight—followed the route weekly. In back rooms, monies were
counted with great care, then poured into canvas sacks, sealed,
tagged, and hefted out into the raw pure daylight and loaded.
One could imagine the bags coming out beneath the broad blue
sky and seeing the light of day for a moment before being borne
up into the dark, cavernous hold, piled up against other bags,
the weighty perplexity of cash compiled against cash; the slug-
gish movement of the truck as it eased out of the parking lot;
the shielded windows, the portals for shotgun muzzles, the
heavy-block weight, the reinforced tires—the imponderable pro-
tective bulkiness of the truck, so fragile and delicate as soon as
it was open to air. That space between point and point, through
which the bags had to travel; that in itself, of course, was the
weak spot, open to human error; the guns belted into holsters,

snapped tight, officious, square-handled; that moment when the money made its way through the morning was the caesura, the quest; the main goal, the main purpose of all the planning, was to find a way into that open air, to coordinate their place in time and space with that of the Brinks truck so that they might, with the simple prompting and the pointing of weapons, provoke the security men, the workers, the hired hacks, to peaceably hand over the bags of money without being shot. That was the original plan laid out; the proviso was that lives would be spared and that it would be a clean, neat operation that went from step to step with the swiftness of exacting precision, an almost mechanical process, but of course it was also brutally clear that one misstep and lives would, as they say, be taken; so it was imperative that they strike at the moment when the cash was nakedly open, when the bags were moving, exposed. The mall had been staked out. She parked there one afternoon, watching from a slouch: ladies moving in and out of the stores, bearing bags, a few men going into Sears for wrenches; one woman with sagging hose, pulling her child along with a stretched arm— overburdened with too many demands, her hair up in a beehive, looking threadbare—swatted the behind of her little boy to move; this woman was evidence, she thought, of what the system does; the system creates burnout, the stress of consumption; the system tears into the ankles; it puffs the ankles up and sends you wobbling along in high heels.

Shooting out in the field in Nebraska, launching shots at a so-called range—really just a pile of old sandbags along one side of a trench—Byron extends his arms, holds his breath, and unleashes a shot that proves him to be the best marksman of them all (because in prep school—a military academy in Tennessee—shooting had been compulsory). When her turn comes she finds pleasure in the gun, solid and heavy with compressed energy as the hammer clicks into place; an enjoyable constriction (in the trigger spring, before the release) sends a bright charge up her arm, and then in answer the kick throws her back on her heels while the blue cloud hangs, reminding her of caps, of firecrackers. (She'll enjoy this same smell later, sifting black powder from a rolled newspaper into galvanized pipes, tapping the wax into place before slipping the fuses through the softness.) Cans. Green glass insulators from old telegraph poles. Wine bottles. Pieces of fence post. She shoots them all and points the gun wildly into the sky and then down, waving the muzzle in Byron's face and laughing until he slugs her hard and she falls back into darkness, only to wake in the trailer with a purple bruise on her brow and pain between her legs.

In the evening the men sit in front of the fire, talking softly, conspiratorially, their words quiet, epigrammatic. When they're planning the heist—as they call it—Byron and August (nicknamed after the month he joined) speak in dainty voices, as if the scheme were an egg to be held with the utmost care. They sketch diagrams on paper—of the mall, the parking lot, the positioning of the truck, the various routes in and out, escape plans and alternates—and then burn the papers ritualistically, poking them into the flames with a stick.

Under the table an electric tingle spreads on her palms when she thinks about the guns and listens as the dogs stop barking, and there is only the rustling of trees, throwing mottled green shadows across the rooms upstairs. The oaks in front of the house have grown close to the screens, touching them, and with the breeze comes a smell from the Hudson that reminds her of summers at Lake George, when her father would come up from the city to visit for the weekends, relaxed, shedding his suit coat, his neck visible, loose-fleshed. Drinkable water, potable, her brother Hank liked to say, trying to get her to sip. You can see all the way to the bottom because it's the purest lake water in the world. Now Hank's in a grave, at Arlington, not far from the eternal flame over J.F.K. (I'm gonna blow it out, he had said, going up to pay his respects when they visited on a family trip.) Each summer, her father took them to the end of the lake to visit Fort Ticonderoga and told them how it had been conquered by a distant relative, Ethan Allen, and his Green Mountain Boys (the land of the dead, Hank had called it—hadn't he?)—and then to a wooded area near the fort where the French had massacred the British, and then the British, a year later, massacred the French. The ghostly aftermath in the wind, the silent vestiges there amid the thin, second-growth forest of quaking aspen and ragged maple. The inaccurately reassembled buttresses. The placards that rang false against the weighty, blood-slicked solidity of history.

Monies to finance the bomb-making! Monies to demolish the status quo! To fight the system you gotta go within and undermine it, kick the scaffolding away. Whatever falls, falls. Those left standing are standing. There are incongruities to any movement, man, errors of judgment, hypocrisies all around, but that's just the way it is, just the way things *are*, Byron says. The day is brilliant and clear with beautiful thick clouds drawing themselves lazily across the sky. Heading south from the hide-out—following Route 9W, the old post road from Albany to New York, to avoid the cops who hang around tollbooths, moving through the old river towns, each presenting itself as brutal proof of the system's failure, with boarded windows and dusty shop fronts and sad men smoking cheap cigars—she listens to Byron, a soft lisp rounding his words as he speaks of the downfall of the system, of tort law, of simultaneous orbital spin reversal, of the Rolling Stones at Altamont, of Lou Reed and the Velvet Underground, of his cohorts and colleagues, those who had failed him and those who hadn't; of the need to locate plain speech, to find a new vernacular, to absolve the transgressions; he speaks in Latin, quoting Horace—"Nay, Xanthias, feel unashamed / That your love is but a servant / Remember, lovers far more famed / Were just as fervent"—while the river through the trees widens and then narrows as they coast the steep grade around Storm King Mountain. (During all of this, August remains silent with his big, meaty hands atop the wheel. He's a quiet man. His words—when he does speak—seem to be pulled from a well by the bucket of his jaw.) Then they're heading down the Palisades Parkway, past the state park, driving carefully, sticking to the speed limit, until they exit to the mall, where they look at their watches and assure themselves—in the bright late-morning light—that the plan is hitchless, locked into simplicity: exploit the open space between the store and the armored truck, the one soft vulnerability in the transportation of great funds. (She imagines the guards on a coffee break, sipping inside the cab of the truck, ignoring the money in the back, bored with the tedium of security work, not so much hoping for a robbery as fully aware that it might be the only way out of the monotonously long days of picking up loot. Perhaps there is some pleasure in staring out the bulletproof glass, far above the fray, and at times peeking through the thick aperture of the arm ports at what seems to be the far-off light of day.) To rob some-one takes a sense that certain borders can be violated, she thinks. In the crux of the act, of course, lies violence. One way or another, the space will be, when they get there, neatly clear of other vehicles. (It's gotta be pure karma, man, Byron had explained. All of the elements have to be aligned. It's as simple as that.) At that moment, a deep, robust smell will emerge from the willow trees that hang delicately over the chain-link fence at the back of the mall. Long, narrow leaves sweeping slightly in the breeze. Byron will point a gun. August will, too.

The two men hauling sacks look up from behind their sun-glasses; one of them has his pistol stuck between his big swing of belly and his belt. The other guy is lean, thin, boyish, nervous-looking, with his hand resting loosely on his gun, as if about to draw, when August says, Stop. Stop.

They agreed, when they were driving east from Nebraska, that the best way to control someone was with one-word com-mands, the way you'd train a dog, not by shouting but rather by speaking softly, with complete authority.

The thin one pauses, his lips parted slightly in a half smile, as if to say: This is the part of the job we expected. It was an even-tuality, resting in the tedium of pickups, banks, Laundromats, furniture warehouses. The tedium of take-out coffee, of casual banter, of heavy traffic—gone. At some point along the line, I was going to come face-to-face with you. Then he lets his hand tighten down on his gun, taking one step forward, which causes August to say stop again. From the car, it all seems remote, as if on a stage. All four actors are forming a rhombus of tension points, a little toe dance from side to side. Then for a minute or so they rest in a frozen stasis. The fat one—from her view— seems wobbly, lifting his arms to reveal long dark stains below his armpits. Stop, Byron says. Step back to the wall. Step back and don't make a move. Then August gives the signal, fluttering his hand behind his back, fluttering some more because:

It is decided, passing over the Mississippi in St. Louis—seeing the arch glinting in the sun, cranking the Rolling Stones, talking about the plan—that the unavoidable cost will be two lives. It is the only way. The discussion that ensues will last all the way across Ohio and into Pennsylvania. The counterargument she puts forth is that it would be just as easy to tie the men up and gag them, and then take them into the culvert behind the mall, down into the weeds by the creek, hidden by the willow branches. But this might allow for a slip-up. A passerby might see us dragging the men (Byron argues); whereas if the men are simply shot against the doorway, they will slump down behind the cover of the parked truck and give us ample time to drive away, unnoticed. The gunshots will present a problem because even with the silencers there might be enough of a report to draw notice, so I think you should honk the car horn, a few sustained toots, and then, in the cover of that sound, we'll shoot both men. August will signal you. He'll wave his hand behind his back.

•

Yeah, there are certain moral objections that can certainly be made, Byron admitted, sipping stale coffee at a truck stop in Clearfield, Pennsylvania. Out the windows, past the bright lights over the gas pumps, beyond the tractor trailers lined up along the curb, strip-mine rigs dug coal, their frames lit like constellations, their car-size maws scooping intergalactic darkness. In the wider moral drama lies the truth, man. The truth is in the wide view. We can't look for it in the minutiae. We've got to keep the larger vision in mind. End of story. End, of the fucking, story. Byron sucked coffee from a spoon and looked out the tall windows. Bathed in a colorless carbon light, the trucks were mulling softly, their engines going while their drivers slept. The topic of death seemed perfectly suited to the truck stop, as it had been to the old shack, back in Nebraska. Death was just one of many objectionable qualities in a landscape littered with antelope horns, the whitewashed skulls of long-dead bison, old truck tires, and, scattered everywhere, fossilized remains so long gone as to be ensconced in meaninglessness. Back there—in the afternoons—huge clouds had ranged up into themselves, towering high until they darkened along the bottoms, flattened out by their own weight, and spit toy forks of lightning that produced audible thunder only if they were listening for it; otherwise, the distance, and the ceaseless wind, devoured everything. Byron put his coffee cup carefully in its saucer, stood up, and went outside to stand in the parking lot. She and August finished their breakfasts. I'm afraid, she said. I'm afraid. I don't think we should kill. I don't think it's right at all. August looked at her and fiddled with his eggs. I want to agree with you, he finally said, nodding at the window, but I have to go with Byron. I can't see leaving them bound and gagged in the ditch, where they might die anyway.

Byron elaborates on the plan: You'll give the horn a good three-second toot to cover the shots (one-apple, two-apple, three-apple), and then another shorter one to make it sound as though you're signaling someone inside to come out. We're a great nation of horn blowers, he adds vis-à-vis the plan, so no one's gonna notice so long as it sounds like a normal, audible transaction, like you're calling to someone to come out, or giving someone a friendly warning. The passing of a signal. My sister's boyfriend used to sound his horn outside our house all the time. Late at night he'd pull up in his car, tap the horn, and I'd look out my bedroom window and watch her sneak out. Then one night he drove up and gave a delicate little signal, just the lightest tap, you could barely call it a honk, and I watched as she skipped down the sidewalk, got in his car, and disappeared into the firmament never to be seen again. So a horn honk is perfectly apropos. No one's gonna notice if you do it right. Later that afternoon, as they drive through eastern Pennsylvania, barreling down toward the Delaware Water Gap, she thinks about the apartment on Park Avenue and how as a young girl she had looked out at the evening traffic, counting the taxis and the buses, listening intently until the mull of noise that normally lay submerged beneath consciousness would dissolve to reveal the sounds of horns. She thought of the view—all the way down to Grand Central if she stuck her head out the window and arched to the right—and the sad elegance of the light, near nightfall in winter. The blueness of the vista, the glory in those lights.

The parking lot is glazed with heat around the car, and near the doorway to the store the men are still stuck in the rhombus of tension, moving slightly in a congruence, a sidelong motion, while August crabs his hand behind his back, signaling away. There isn't really fear inside her; there's nothing except a bag of air inflating against her rib cage, and her fingers light on the metal horn band that makes a half circle around the steering wheel, unwilling to push—no, it's not that simple. She conspired with herself to avoid making a sound that would cover the shots, and she knows what she'll do next, and she does it, backing the car up and then heading off across the parking lot, not too fast, but fast enough, naturally, focusing her eyes straight ahead and trying to picture Hank in her mind, his boyish face in his uniform, the collar tight up against his neck, and his smile, bright and hopeful, as he tells her not to worry, that he'll be back in the summer and they'll go to Lake George together just like the war never happened; trying to keep that vision in front of her and her hands steady, she drives onto the main road and heads east, while a wild posse of police cars— old ones with rounded fenders and single dome lights—roars west in a fury of rage and torment.

In Nebraska, smoking cigarettes in the shack and acting tough—with Byron in a leather cowboy hat cured from the sun and salt-stained, with the stitching coming loose where the crown was attached and the brim curled up in front—she let August bleach her hair (he had a sister who'd taught him how), and for a few days she felt like Marilyn Monroe in *The*

Misfits—rugged, rustic, embraced not only by fear but also by something deeper, a landscape urgently, almost sexually, unforgiving. She felt during those days a new physicality; her body seemed born anew as her thighs slid against the denim. Her hips turned bony, hard, and she lurched like a cowpoke when she walked. They strove for a certain élan, a style to the mission, as if they might capture the spirit of Bonnie and Clyde—not the actual historical characters, who seemed messy and dirty, not to mention dead, but the ones portrayed by Warren Beatty and Faye Dunaway in the movie, hazed by the lens filter, eternally laughing and skipping their way through bank robberies and gas station holdups until they were devoured again and again by their love for each other and by the fate—a hail of bullets—that was waiting for them along that road in Louisiana. She felt an elegance emerge, not just in her movements but in her posture, her stance, the way she stood on the earth, facing the horizon, alone on the ridge, while the men worked on the plan back in the shack. Sometime around then a guy named Jamake appeared, a local Sioux Indian who arrived one afternoon on his motorcycle and offered to lend a hand. He looked squint-eyed, walked with a slight limp, and made smirking, knowing looks behind Byron's back. When they hiked together, he put his hand against her back in a way that was unthreatening, keeping it fanned out high near her shoulders as he told her about plants that were edible and freely available from the land, prairie turnips and Jerusalem artichokes, and in the southern ranges the leaves of the lechuguilla, which had to be cut up and baked properly for several days. You don't cook them exactly right, they're as hard as bayonet blades, he said. There are things like that all over the place, man, things that have to be tempered under a steady heat for days on end or they're just another thorny plant and not worth shit. Up on the tattered edge of the ridgeline they sat and talked, and he told her that he had been born in Utah and lived on the lam from the lawmen who were after him for some activities he had performed as part of the movement. And she told him about her early days living with Byron near San Francisco, in a bungalow with a view of the Pacific. She told him about her childhood in New York, with her businessman father, sailing toy boats in the Central Park pond. She did not talk about Hank, or about the war, or about those things that drove her to join the underground. There was a perplexity between them that was pleasurable and right. The conversation was limited. He withheld his condemnation of the white boys making plans down in the shack. He did not say—as he obviously wanted to say—that these were foolish rich kids playing a game and afraid of real confrontation; these were kids couched in money and self-righteousness and an old sense of propriety that was unearned and therefore unwarranted; these were boys who had been taught a predestination that went against the truth of nature. He did not advise her to ignore their orders—except in the way he looked when she told him of their plans (askance, squinting his eyes and spitting to the side). Instead he told her that he was pure fuckin' AIM, nothing more and nothing less—American Indian Movement all the way, from Wounded Knee to Wounded Knee—while he fixed her with the gracious element of his eyes, dark blue in one but white and cloudy in the other. A sucker punch caused that a few years back, he said. I was walking along the road, and a man came up on his chopper and begged directions. I showed him the way to Highway 29, and in gratitude he struck me from behind with an implement, a crowbar or tire iron. He took that side of my sight but he gave me vision, pure Indian vision. And now I see the

way I was meant to see even though, truth be told, I was actually born with the name Bill Winston, outside of Chicago, in
Oak Park, and, until I reclaimed my real name, I was nothing
but a plain old white man. Then he told her about the standoff
with the state troopers somewhere out in the Great Basin, and
how men and women (himself included) had blocked a supply
road to a research center where the white man took advantage
of the vast emptiness, securing a parcel, cordoning it with
barbed wire and high fences and security checkpoints. You see,
at night there were ghostly casts of light in the sky that killed
the stars, he said. There were the appearances of strange flying
craft that devoured the migrating birds and cut holes across the
heavens, rending them apart so you could see the guts of the
universe. So in protest we lay in the road and let the police drag
the women into the culvert and the men, who gave no struggle,
away into the system of justice you've created. You see, man, the
sky was weeping and strange, and it was sorrowful and purple,
like that bruise there on your head. So now the universe is a
fucking mess. Then he kissed her, and she kissed him back, and
he said, It's fucked up. There just isn't a fucking thing we can do
about it, man. And then he leaned his head against her shoulder
and wept quietly. When they met again up on the ridge, one
final time, early in the morning with the dew on the grass and
soft cobwebs on their cuffs, they made love quickly with their
pants down around their ankles so that only their bellies seemed
united, hot, eager. Byron was down below, packing up, loading
stuff into the car while August checked the camp to make sure
they weren't leaving any clues behind. There was a fire in which
the papers were being burned, sending up a trickle of black
smoke into the morning sky, which was shrouded in a thin white
haze around the edges but beginning to turn blue overhead. The

guy named Jamake was moving softly over her, and she had her eyes open and was looking into his good one, trying to see something, and when he came she noticed that he didn't blink but instead looked directly at her until he leaned down to kiss her with lips that tasted of ash, dew, and smoke. The wind was twining his hair around her lips and cheeks. Then, from down below, Byron was giving the horn a toot, a soft, short report that said: We're ready to go now, and you're gonna have to leave that ridge and come down from there, leave that Indian asshole behind and get in the fucking car. Up on the ridge she didn't move for a minute as she lay against Jamake, who was reaching down, wiping her softly with a bandana, cleaning her up so that she might go off into the world. The car horn was sounding again, angry and persistent. It seemed there was nothing she could do but get up, smooth down her jeans, and hike back, holding tight to the side of the narrow trail, stepping carefully along the ridge where it fell off into nothing, a dusty wash of stones just starting to catch the full brunt of daylight.

The part when the guns go off and the horn doesn't honk: There is a random anarchy of the moment—amid the yelling, the shouts, the fear—smoothed by the swaying willow branches, which make a soft, almost broom-sweep sound against the chain-link fence; men face one another with weapons drawn in a standoff, posited, posted, tensions created; the wiry guard is stark-still, frozen, producing more fear in Byron because the immutability, the cold posturing seems—and this is a quick mind-flash—inhuman, his eyes unmoving. The larger guy sways on his heels, both arms out with his gun. The swaying is imperceptible to everyone except August; August, too, is moving a little, and he feels, amid the conjoining of many sensations, an awareness of his weight and heft, hanging over his belt, tightly packed in his legs, as a significant disadvantage. He is a large target. But he is too involved in the tension, in the urgent dynamic before him, to think too much about this fact. The entire thing resolves itself down into those positions, into that tension, into the guns drawn and the directions they are pointed while, from the car, from her vantage, she watches and tries to see and sees only one side, one angle of the action: two men dressed in uniforms of pale olive, with stitched patches indicating their names, one fat and one thin, standing fearfully with their guns out, beneath the direct implications of the noon sun; Byron and August out of sight, positioned almost behind the truck, just their guns visible, pointing; the bags of money weighty and heavy at the feet of the larger man; all frozen there for a moment in the fear and agony until there is the flash of muzzle fire and then—in what seems to be a modulated time/space, not slow motion but rather something else, a kind of compact glimmering shimmer of movement—the fat man falls to the side, collapsing under the weight of his torso as his knees give, falling to the ground and then bowing down, prayerfully, his dark oil-slicked hair glinting in the light and his scalp bright red with sweat until another bullet hits and the top of his skull flowers with bone and spray; then the other man falls, too, his lean, slim body folding over sidelong and leathery; his own bones frail and delicate so that he appears to come down to the earth with a sliding motion, like a leaf in the wind, crumpling over himself.

All noise and commotion held off for a moment until she realized that she *had* honked the horn and was leaning on it too long; that behind her in the parking lot a lady, pushing a cart, had paused to look over and was coming toward her; that she was still on the horn, the sound bending and turning in on itself; and the men were now waving to her to stop, lugging the bags in her direction, Byron with two to balance himself and August just two-fisting the bags in one hand while he waved his gun wildly in the other; she realized that behind the lady, far off at the entryway of the lot, there was the flash of red light indicating a cop coming, and then another flash of light behind it, all under that bright noon sun with the swish of willows to her left and beneath that, down past the chain-link, a musky earthen smell of the river that seemed to bring the whole scene—the cracked dirty macadam, the green Dumpsters stenciled with white lettering, the drab back doorways (each painted a russet color)—into some congruence with the natural world, the everlasting world that would eternally outlast these stupid sinning willful men who were dying by their own clock. So when she backed up and around to escape she was thinking of that smell, and of the river, and she turned too fast and struck the lady with the car, clattering her load, spilling her cart and sacks of groceries and knocking her to the ground. (She was an older lady, not so enfeebled but frail-looking, in a long smock-like coat, pale yellow, with eyeglasses of wire rims and a dusky-looking hairdo, pulled up; she was one of those old ladies who went to the beauty parlor weekly and had her bouffant arranged and neatened and listened to the patter and gossip but with a certain reserve; she was originally from St. Louis and had a certain composure that came from the Middle West and still, at times, found herself strangely and oddly out of place in her New Jersey town, right on the border of New York.) The men shouted to her to stop and not to go, holding the bags up and then coming over and trying to stand in front of the car to block her way and to limit her options to two: to drive over them and kill them or to stop and let them aboard, to hold off; Byron had his gun forward and was trying to find her face through the glare of the windshield and she knew, right then, seeing him, that if need be he would shoot her and be done with it, because he had shown, in his beatings, that he had the capacity to hurt without thought and that his body was at times out of his control. He held the gun out and sighted along it and said stop and she did; she did stop for a moment, until she continued into her reverse turn, moving the car around the lady, who was trying to clamber up, and then swinging forward so that she was facing the police cars, which were wending around among the parking spaces, looking for something to lock on to, their sirens wailing loudly now. But they didn't spot her, really; they were moving around to the right, to the south, and coming along the back side of the lot, coming around and heading toward the armored truck but not seeing her, apparently; she was now driving forward, slowly, not too fast—to avoid attention—but just fast enough to look leisurely. In a matter of one or two minutes she was out on the main road heading south; she was blending in with traffic and silently congregating with the others out shopping, running errands—the plumbing trucks, the delivery vans, the women loaded up with kids. She went from the scene behind the mall with death and mayhem to something else instantly; on the other side of the meridian a cluster of police cars—sirens wailing, valiant in their formation—passed quickly and unaware. She got on the old road heading north; it would be the long route but it would be safer, probably, and although she hadn't heard all the details of the plan and was kept from knowing them, she did know one thing, and that was that the old road—which went up through the depression-ravaged Hudson River towns—would probably be safer.

·

She would begin to look for the house; she would track it down
intuitively. What she knew was only what she remembered from
coming down; there was an old lumberyard in the town where
she would turn right, gloomy old storefronts empty of wares
and falling into disrepair, a store that sold party items and gags
and magic tricks wholesale, and then, after that, an old public
library, stately and grand up along a sloping hill. There she
would turn down the narrow road that, from what she remembered, sloped toward the river; at a street called Ross she would
turn right into another road, narrow and elegant; she would go
back to the old house and sit alone and find a way into something else, she thought; the weeds outside would give under the
wind and sway softly and it would be beautiful; the soft tarry
smell would arrive from the road; the house would heave and
creak softly under the hot sun, and she would go from room to
room and examine them for clues, for some long-lost remnants
of the life that had gone on there before it was reduced to broken glass, to long cracked wounds in the plaster that showed the
lath behind; she would bow down on all fours to God; she
would find herself in the basement amid the dusty light from
the window wells and the smell of heating oil and the earthen
floor, compacted into the corner there, under the old table, in
the cobwebby recess she knew was there because she had gone
with the men when they explored the house and Byron had
bonged on the old tank while August, heaving his weight
around, did a dance and sang "Sympathy for the Devil"; she'd
feel an urge to spend the rest of eternity there in the dark and
the cool, because right now, driving in the car, her desire was to
get away from the bright sun and the sensation of the wild passing landscape that seemed so surfaced with light that it was

impossible to look at; then in the morning if she saw some kind of new light from the window, sifting down through the motes of dust, she might go up and out again into a new world, entering with bare feet and walking the dew-wet road down to the river, where maybe if all was right and the world was back into some order she would find a cool cove loaded with myrtle and elderberry, and sit and watch the currents move and the boats far off. Maybe there, in that place, she would be located and identified and brought forth into the world of men and justice the way Byron said she would; then fate would play its hand and she'd be where she was intended to be, she thought, holding the wheel, driving carefully, avoiding speed traps, passing through a town named Newburgh that seemed depleted of all life and grace except where a few old grand homes hung on, big and robust, kept up nicely; she was a good and careful driver when calm, and she knew that one way or another she would get back to the hideout and fulfill the vision she had of how this whole thing would come to an end.

All Wondering

Let's say the beach erodes fifty yards in at the rate of a yard a year, give or take a few. By the time the Atlantic reaches his body—by then nothing but bones, if even that—it won't matter, Carl said. Unless his body works its way up and out, like a seed in reverse. You know, remember those old biology films showing in slow-mo stop-action the way certain seeds wiggle into the ground, taking advantage—I guess that's the way to put it—of their natural designs in relation to the winds, wending down until they're deep enough to root. All manipulation of form in conjunction with nature. Except, knowing Dad, his body might respond the other way, twisting up and out of the sand until some hiker comes upon a toe, or a brow. Just imagine his body emerging under a moonless sky with only the sweep of the light-house for company. Just imagine old Pop, old Dad, wondering where the hell he is, or at least theoretically wondering because presumably his wondering days are over. All his wondering has been relegated to some other realm, in the best of circum-stances, or to the void, in the worst. Just imagine his bald pate exposed to the salt air—just about impossible to see in the sand, or a toe, already mentioned, coming up and out of the razor grass, or the brambles, and moving, depending on the freeze-thaw cycles, too slow for the human eye, but over time—if you could see the slowed-down action speeded up—wiggling softly in the manner of resurrected flesh, as one imagines it, Carl argued; or maybe even rising up, stiff-jointed, like a marionette in the quiet of the off-season, jerked around by invisible strings stretching up to the Holy Father. Or it's just as easy to imagine the body doing the seed routine properly, Carl said, his voice suddenly husky and deep, caught up in a madness that came not so much from Dad's body, it seemed, but from the lack of logic his argument was taking, gathered up into the sack of his grief, his voice barely audible. Burn the bastard. Freeze his ass. Shoot him into space. Plunge him into the center of the earth. At times, his thoughts, like perfectly out-of-phase sound waves, nullified themselves for a moment into a pure silence. Or the body might dig itself down into the soft pliancy, the liquescence of sand, yearned by gravity, twisting itself with the contraction of drying sinew and cartilage in the bright fall heat, during those clear Cape days before Thanksgiving (Carl said) when the snap of leaf mold and the scent of musket smoke hangs in the air, at least theoretically, because Miles Standish musket smoke is still up there, man, somewhere. (Carl lifted his hand and pointed vaguely in the direction of First Encounter Beach, where, almost four hundred years ago, the first hostile American shots were fired.) The corpse might spiral down (Carl said) until, with toes pointed and head haut, it drove hard to the bed-rock. (He forcefully landed on each syllable, dividing the word into two.) Then, when he looked up at me with the mute, inac-cessible eyes of a man sealed in the vacuum of stalemate, I saw that he was a chip off the old block. What Dad had contained, he contained. Now the original block was just solid matter, and

Carl was the live chip leaning into his shovel to rest, looking out over the Atlantic while between us came a mutual agreement—unspoken—that the hole would have to go down at least fifteen feet to give the body a chance, to find a depth of equalization (as Carl later called it, groping retrospectively for the proper phrase), where the forces drawing our father up would meet on equal terms with the forces drawing him down. From that point it was all digging and digging, widening the hole against the sliding sand, working furiously, one taking a turn with the shovel while the other dug with his hands, working for several hours until we got down fifteen feet, stopping only on occasion to rest, to look out over the roar of surf—big, lazy-edged waves coming in on an angle, rolling themselves against the hook of the beach from one end to the other, each producing a shush sound from right to left while the sun, for its part, sank against the sharp horizon—invisible, over the verge behind us, paring away at whatever light remained of the day.

The Spot

Jack Dunhill, a.k.a. Bone, a.k.a. the Bear, a.k.a. Stan New-
hope, a.k.a. Winston Leonard, a.k.a. Michigan Pete, a.k.a. Bill
Dempsey, a.k.a. Shank, said, Not those waves but that little
pucker on the surface out there is where the Cleveland water
supply is drawn in, right there, and if you were to dump enough
poison on that spot you'd kill the entire city in one sweep.
Believe me, I've thought it out. You'd just have to hit right there,
he said, pointing again, and then he turned to examine her gaze,
and in doing so presented his face, weathered from years of
picking blueberries and cherries in Michigan, and, after that, a
merchant marine gig during Vietnam. You see, the water is
unsuspecting until it hits that spot. It has no idea it's gonna be
collected, drawn under the streets, cleaned up, and piped into
homes. Not a clue. But when it touches that suck, its future
vanishes. No chance of becoming a wave after that, no kissing
the shore and yearning back out into the lake. Instead, it ends
up pooled on somebody's lawn, or slipping down a throat,
or spooned into a bowl of baby cereal. That's the mystery of
chance. One minute you're one thing, the next you're another,
and choice had nothing at all to do with it. He paused, pointed

one last time at the spot, shook himself free of his reverie, and pulled her close while she searched the water, tried to find the spot, and, failing to do so, said, I see it. I do. It's right where you said it would be.

. . . All this while killing time in Cleveland, waiting for the Mansfield john to show up to collect the girl, because against all odds he had sent payment in advance for an evening of pleasurable escort after succumbing to Shank's well-polished pitch:

The girl's name is Meg. Hell, name her whatever you want, but I'd like you to call her Meg when you greet her for the first time, my friend. Said girl being in the prime of her youth, fresh as a daisy and raring to go. She'd practically escort you for free if I weren't around to mediate her desires, my friend, he said from a phone booth outside Ypsilanti, watching the girl as she sat in the car, fixing her face in the mirror. The Mansfield john's number had come from a list of potential clients he'd been keeping, names and numbers whispered to him as he and Meg rambled aimlessly around the Great Lakes. OHIO MEN IN NEED, it said at the top in block lettering. Below were six names. He'd tried four of them already, with no luck, but this time he felt the guy taking the bait—a sense of urgency formed at the other end of the line as the Mansfield john succumbed to the image he had painted: a bright young girl entwined in a skein of sexual confusion, open to just about anything. A girl born out of the loins of Akron, smothered by a father's touch, and then cast out to fend for herself. (He'd left out the boring details: the way he had come upon her small body curled up, asleep, beneath an overpass outside Port Huron; the long journey they'd taken around the rim of the state of Michigan, following the mitten, staying as close as possible to the waterline. He'd left out her delicate neckline and the shallow hopelessness of her gaze and the way he'd educated her in how to make use of her flesh to earn funds. He'd left out his former religious training at the Grand Rapids Bible Institute and the way God had failed to give him a precise indication of His Will.)

After that, he'd begun to zero in on a price, speaking to the image he had conjured of a somewhat dainty man in neat trousers, with the kind of studied, dreamy comportment you'd expect from a farmer who had gone into the seed business and left fieldwork behind for good; there was a hint of yokel in the Mansfield john's voice, a bit of hick around his tongue tempered by churchgoing and Sunday-school teaching. Yes, there was most certainly some Bible study in the formality of his elocutions, and there was fear in the amplitude of his voice—just loud enough to sound natural. In the phone booth, Shank imagined Mansfield as a man with neat hair, parted clean on the left-hand side, held with a shellac of brilliantine, cut tight above the ears. His wife would be in the family room watching television, aware of her husband in the kitchen, maybe even listening in on his side of the conversation, which to her would seem naturally cryptic because he often made deals on the phone, talking about seed prices, the best hybrids to plant, the way to intercrop carrots with corn. With this in mind, Shank took care when the dickering began and told Mansfield, Just say soy if you're going to bid lower on Meg, and alfalfa if we hit the magic number. Eventually the john said, softly, Yes, alfalfa is the way to go because it's a versatile crop, alfalfa will do just fine in your soil if you're lucky with the weather, and Shank said, Good, we've got a deal and you'll be saving this little girl's life, Mansfield, you understand, because she's putting money away for college after being kicked out of her home for no good reason. Then he instructed the man where and when to meet, adding, Just give us a nod. You'll see us standing around outside the Holiday Inn, and then go on and check in and I'll send her up to you. You'll know us when you see us. I'll be the one with the big shoulders, and she'll be the one with the sweet derriere.

Here we are, Shank thought (or maybe said) outside the hotel, waiting out yet another john delayed by his guilt and his doubts and the time it takes to check his morality at the door, driving north, praying for forgiveness, taking a rain check on his deeper principles while the dull fields fly eagerly past the bug-speckled windows. As Mansfield drives, alone in the car, his face will be composed—the same look he might have when teaching his Sunday-school class—as he reaches up once or twice to straighten his cuffs, or his tie, and assures himself that if he maintains a certain formality he'll be able to justify anything he might do in this good world. When he gets to the hotel, he'll be so enthralled by his own desire—acute, as solid as carved stone—that the rest of his life, the house and the business and his upstanding place in the community, will become nothing but a small white dot behind him, zipping away like the last of an old television image.

A bolo tie at his throat, fresh-pressed plaid shirt tucked smartly into his chinos, the john will unchain the door, let it swing open, throw his arms wide, and say, Come on in, Meg, offering up a room truncated and narrow, papered in gold foil, periscoping to a view of Lake Erie from fifteen stories up. She'll go directly to the window and stay there, with her back to him, as long as possible, looking out, trying to fashion some drama.

From the violent johns she's learned that it's best to build up an assemblage of gestures, somewhat vaudevillian and slapstick, around the act itself in order to preempt the hard, cold dynamics that otherwise set in naturally. (She would've got that from her father, an old tool-and-die guy; an awareness of the importance of the fine gradients, of using a micrometer, measure twice, cut once, and all that . . .) Most johns were as hard as tungsten, as square inside as an unworked block. Behind her, Mansfield will cough a couple of times, unhitch his belt, and then approach her hesitantly. Beneath his facade of neat and upstanding morals will be a horrible goatlike presence, a humping energy that will arrive musky and damp, pressing up against her, moaning, reaching around to tweak her breasts. That much is certain. This john's a connoisseur of dry, Shank had warned her. He likes it sandpapery and rough, no lubrication, none, nada.

As Shank waited for her down in the hotel lobby, he began to feel himself edging into pure speculation. He knew little about what really went on up in the room, but he had a basic idea and he could imagine, in general terms, how she coped. Most likely she'd:

1. Find a crass rigidity, all bone and sinew, in the brashness of survival.
2. Abolish the formality of her own flesh. Reduce herself down to an essence—hips, the arch of her foot and shoulder blades, the part in her hair, the fine down on her earlobes, the nape of her neck.
3. Assume a protoplasmic mobility; the creep of the protozoan, one-celled hydra, primal and original and eager to consume itself for lunch.

In due course, Mansfield will tell her that he sells seed and some heavy equipment wholesale, just outside of town proper, and then he'll let his pants fall to the floor, step out of them, and move behind her as he places his cold, bloodless hands around her belly and tries to turn her while she resists slightly, and then some more, until he has to use a little force, and then they'll do a give-and-take shuffle to the bed, where he'll push her down and take her clothing off a bit at a time until finally they'll be doing it, and then he'll completely embody that goat-like carnality, grunting and groaning, while she keeps her eyes closed and concentrates on the spot Shank had pointed out to her on the water earlier, and she'll think about how it would feel to be devoured by darkness and then spat out somewhere, startled and renewed, fresh and tight from a spigot into a bucket or out onto a lush lawn somewhere pleasant—yes, she'll use that image, hold on to it, and it will make things easier for her, he thought down in the lobby, waiting for her to emerge from the elevator, which she did, about forty-five minutes later, raising her hand to adjust her hair, glancing around for him with a bit too much eagerness.

There was something in her face, a slackness in her jaw that foretold the confession she'd give an hour later, driving through the moonlit suburb of Lakewood, speaking softly, saying: He had that string tie on the whole time, and it kept bugging me. You know, those cold metal tips kept brushing me, and it was like they were saying, Here I am, yank me. We're ready to go. Just grab hold. Cross the line, he said. Not out loud, but with his hands and his you-know-what. I said no. He struck me and said, Cross it. I said no. He hit me again. Then those strings told me: Draw me tight. And so I did. I did. It took all my might. I dug a knee into his ribs, tightened the bolo tie around his throat, and rode him like a bronco until he stopped moving, she said.

Shank could just barely make out the shape of her face in the pale Ohio light. Go on. Go on, he said, and she said, Well, what do you want to hear? Give me the nitty-gritty, he said. Give me the sick parts that this country ain't ready for, the bits folks would never believe. He waited, listening to the engine shudder. Well, she said, his teeth popped out during the fight. His bridge, I guess you'd call it, the four front ones, and when I was done I popped them into my mouth and said, What's up, doc? You didn't, he said, feeling the laugh come up from his ribs and then listening as she laughed in response.

Eventually they were up on the beach road, passing sensible homes, locked tight and frowning out at the lake with mute but unshaded windows while the first light came along the edge of the lake and he explained to her how even Erie would ignite if you touched a match to it correctly, and then he rambled on, trying to stop himself at first, about the time he'd witnessed the Cuyahoga River burn, a calico blanket of shimmering flames elbowing its way into the heart of Cleveland, and how the sight of it had changed everything and made him aware that his calling wasn't with the Lord, because there hadn't been a single recognizable sign of prophecy in that water, even as it burned.

After a swing up to Detroit for no good reason except to pay off a gambling debt and to cast a glance at Lake St. Clair, they headed east along the dreary tedium of Canada, Highway 401, the staggering dull flatness and repetition. This part of Canada's nothing but a feeble reflection of U.S. glory, he said. Then he carried on about old draft-dodger buddies who'd gone nuts from missing the American stuff. Guys who hallucinated burger joints, strip clubs, and billboards behind their eyelids. I avoided that. I skirted that issue, he said. I went into the merchant marine to get around running to Canada, and I got around it easy while my buddies went over and came back fucked-up, or dead. Do I feel the guilt that comes from that? I certainly do. Do I live each day pondering it? I certainly do. Do I lament the way history chewed my best buddies up? I certainly do. Do I wonder at the great forlorn gravity of the way things went in the past? I most certainly do. Do I spend my days in a state of total lament? I certainly do. Do I tell the same old threadbare stories over and over as a way to placate the pain that is stuck between my rib bones? I do indeed. Am I just another lost sixties soul who dropped one tab too many and can't extricate myself from a high? I certainly am. And then, from that point, he kept talking, unable to help himself, until his discourse expanded (while she dozed and slept fitfully, rising from her dreams to catch fragments of his voice) and he fell into a reverie and told a long story as he drove, keeping close to the speed limit because the Mounties were out, their hats aslant. Here's the story, verbatim, as he told it:

There was this guy named Ham. This was just after my buddy Billy-T came back from his first tour of duty. You had to surmise Ham's story, because otherwise he was pretty much a blank slate. A big guy, the son of a pipe fitter from the Upper Peninsula, he was living in that shantytown I told you about, the old hobo hangout near the Kalamazoo River, a spot beneath the railroad tracks, not far from a gravel pit. Anyway, Ham had this wigwam setup, an assemblage of old sheet iron, tar paper, birch bark, leather, nylon, deer hides, and bearskins laid over the original Potawatomi wigwam frame, arched branches twined with petrified deer hide, and the old smoke hole, too—and there was another shack, which had originally been a sweat lodge or something. You went in and smoked some hash and listened for the spirits to call. And they did call, man. Those spirits came in all forms and sizes and said things you'd never forget, at least not for a while.

Anyway, Ham had this girl, Maggie, a street kid from Detroit, a real looker, with those baby blues, bright blond hair, and a lispy little pair of lips that had trouble around polysyllabic words. Naturally, I took a shine to her, but she was Ham's, and you couldn't so much as look her way without getting him on your case. I snuck a glance anyhow, when I could. One day, I took her by the hand and led her down to the river and told her I'd baptize her right there if she wanted, and she said she did, go on, do it to me, make me clean or whatever. My study at the Bible institute was a year or so behind me then, but the words were still around, and I could still utter them in a convincing way. Full immersion, I told her. The works. Right down to an evocation of the Holy Spirit, which would pass into her soul, and so on and so forth, and her soul flying upward, skyward, I said, and so on and so forth. I admit, I laid it on thick, talking about the purity of her heart this, and the salvation of the soul that, and so on and so forth, and she listened to me attentively while her hands, tiny things, fluttered like hummingbirds sipping from her ears. Even now, when I think about it, I can imagine them fluttering on my shoulders and breastbone. (Here he lifted his hands from the steering wheel and waved his fingers.) Anyway, the Kalamazoo was one of the most polluted rivers in the world at the time. You could've walked across it if you'd had the will to do so. That sounds like an exaggeration, I know, but it was loaded with pulp waste from the paper mills, along with whatever Checker Cab felt like adding to the mix. In any case, I led her through the bush to the shore and we stood there looking at the water. This was early evening, or maybe dawn, or maybe early afternoon, late fall, perhaps, but a warm day for sure. The sky tried to reflect itself in the water but failed. Clouds and trees fell against the surface and were lost forever. The fish in the Kalamazoo begged for the hook. You'd flip them onto the shore and they'd flex their gills as a way of saying thanks. A few hardy bugs stalked the surface, yanking their gummy feet. You'll do better, I mean gracewise, without those garments, I told her.

Meanwhile, during all of this, Ham was in his wigwam, sleeping. He slept like a mule. You could hear his snores all the way down to the shore. At least I thought you could. I knew he'd eventually get up, find her gone, and start looking. I knew he'd come down the trail noisily, heaving from side to side, unsteady on his feet, coughing and wheezing, because he was a grizzly of a man, and he snorted and snuffled even when he was still. You wanted to give him fair warning if you came up to him from behind. One was inclined to wear a bear bell around the guy.

Anyway, in her full naked glory there was a shame in her that made her put her hands up, and then down, and then up. I said, I'm going to hold you under and speak the words, and you'll be down there in the depths, where it's dark and dreary, amid the detritus and waste for a moment, and you'll panic, most likely, feeling my hand here, I said, putting my hand on the back of her head. But you must resist the panic because I'll keep you under just as long as it takes me to say the words. Then I'll release you and you'll come up sputtering into newborn light brighter than anything you've seen before. And she said, I'm right for it, I'm in need, I've got blemishes that must be washed away, and I said, Good, good, you're ready. But one more thing. When you see that newborn light, take a long look before it fades when your eyes adjust. You only get a glimpse before it goes away, and then you have to rely on memory, and if your memory isn't strong you'll lose your grip on salvation. Then I took her into the water and started, pushing her under, and at some point I heard Ham on his way down, heaving through the brush. He must've seen me through the trees. What did he see? A man gripping his girl's head, holding her down while she wiggled with the Holy Spirit, splashing a froth into the air. Naturally, from his vantage, he misconstrued my actions and became wild with rage, dancing his way bowlegged through the brambles, held back only by his fear of water. Ham's terror of water was incredible. He could hardly find it in himself to splash his own face from the tap. He found brushing his teeth impossible. You could see his fear in the way he went in up to his toes and then backed out quickly. There were huge forces at play. He'd gone up against them as far as he could, and then he drew a line. He cursed the water, the river, and then yours truly. Against this backdrop, I tried to keep to the task at hand, and if anyone's to blame for my failings, for holding her under a beat too long, it's Ham himself for proving such a distraction. Timing is everything when it comes to the work of baptism. One wrong move and God enters the world at a weird angle. Take my word for it. I kept to the task at hand. After I released her body to the currents, Ham raced along the shore. I can't account for her spirit, but her body swung in wide windmill loops as it was drawn downstream, just out of Ham's reach. For a moment he stood still, quivering in a force field between his rage toward me and his lust for her. Lust won the prize, and he moved downstream, trying to lure her in with the end of a branch. But the currents were too strong.

Long story short, I went back to Ham's wigwam and sacked his food. Long story short, I ate his food while he followed her body all the way to Lake Michigan, where he stood on the shore and rolled his shoulders, as if bracing for a fight. He stood on the shore and bellowed. He was a grand, operatic bellower. His voice spiraled out over the water, as if blown from a conch shell. A big fat bellow that came five miles up the river to his wigwam, where by the time the sound got to me it was weak and feeble but still as clear as day. I sat, held off on my chewing as long as I could, and listened, clenching my teeth against the ringing in my ears and the soft breeze that was coming through the leaves as evening approached. I was happy, because when the evening light met the Kalamazoo it did so on equal terms, and then for a while, until night fell and it was too dark to see, the river looked clean and even drinkable, Meg, as pure as anything you've seen in the world up until now.

He talked and then fell silent and then talked some more, until a few hours later they were in Niagara Falls and he nudged her awake so she could see the mist plume over the horizon. Then they drove along the river and up to the observation station and got out to stretch their legs. That river goes the wrong fucking way, it goes north instead of south, he explained, taking her hand. Then he climbed onto the fence and sat, patting the wooden railing. It goes against the grain of gravity heading that way, Meg. And it did. To their right the Niagara's water tore along the bank, groped hard, forming small eddies in which leaves and bits of trash pooled; to their left all fury and wonder until the river got close to the edge and then grew smooth and calm, thin with hesitation. You'll be able to walk out there if you're careful enough and stick with the harder surface near the edge, he said, and if I tell you to do it, you'll do it, won't you? You'll step right out there on your beautiful little feet when I give you the command, and you'll be just fine.

One more textbook case of discard and loss, another suicide fished out of the waters. Bodies were pushed to the bottom initially—for a few minutes—and then, unless snagged on the rocks below, they bobbed up and twirled around, unable to catch the outflow, which made it easy for the man named Kit Wilson, who took his Zodiac out with the collecting nets, to catch hold of her body and draw it up against the hull. Another slipper, he thought. Another foolish tourist who got too close. Another drunkard unable to resist the lure of danger. Another kid who went in too deep and couldn't get out of the rage. Another American testing the edge. (Canadians rarely went over.) Another girl skinny-dipping with her boyfriend, swimming too far out into the tangle of currents, taking the long trip down with plenty of time to think over her life and to consider the mistakes she'd made in one form or another. Maybe she simply couldn't live up to the expectations that life had, and decided that this was the best way to go, majestic and grand, united with the great drive of the water that had been coming over this escarpment for a million years (with the exception of that wonderful time, years ago, when just a trickle came over the scarred jawbone of rock while the rest of the mighty river was surprised to find itself diverted through the power-plant intake pipes). It seemed that at least once a year the same girl came over the falls to give him a bit role in the large drama that would culminate when the news crews showed up and asked him to speak. His Canuck voice would be clear and exact: We don't know where she came from. No idea why she did it. The falls aren't something to fool with. And, No, I don't get used to pulling them out like this.

He fished her out and saw that she was maybe fourteen or fifteen, with a thin, malformed rump, tiny arms, and a bruised face, cut along her brow, from which stared a pair of mute blue eyes. Her lips were pulled back in a grimace, exposing a gap between her two front teeth. Looking down at the body, flexing along with the hull, he got a hint of her story. (Later he'd hear her name, Meg Allen, and learn that her history could be traced back as far as a hotel in Cleveland, where she had murdered a seed dealer from a place called Mansfield, and then a bit farther back, to a hell-on-earth childhood in Akron.) Whatever produced these bodies with regularity would go on, he thought. If there was a way to stop it, it had long ago been forgotten. He held the tiller and got the motor going full throttle and watched as the wake dug surprisingly straight and clean out of the torment. He loved the feel of the boat when its stern cut deep and, in turn, the bow lifted toward the sky, slapping over the waves. He loved the way the wake spread itself out—even in the foam and rage—and how, when he was past the wash-up, as they called it, the water gathered itself into order and smoothed quickly, as if eager to be done with all the noise and to get back to a more settled existence on the way down to the whirlpool, where it would spin mindlessly for a few minutes before being released into the relative calm of the river as it headed toward the merciful breadth of Lake Ontario.

Reading Chekhov

He was a thirty-five-year-old part-time student at Union Seminary. In four years he would be the minister of a church up the Hudson, in a place called Sneden's Landing. But at this time he was working for an interdenominational insurance organization in an office building on Claremont Avenue, just off Broadway. The view from his window was spectacular, stretching all the way up to the George Washington Bridge and the Palisades beyond. When the carillon played in the tower of Riverside Church, across the street—the individuated notes of the bells smearing together by the time they reached him—he sometimes felt its vibrations, spreading his fingers out against the glass.

She commuted in from a town thirty miles up the river and worked two floors down as an insurance adjuster. Steeples that have toppled in storms, she explained. You know, church fires and the like. Midwestern churches are always burning, being rebuilt, and then burning again. I think of church fires as a kind of civic right of passage. You know, bucket brigades passing hand-to-hand. Then there are lawsuits, of course, elderly slips and so on. You'd be surprised at how often people stumble during Communion. But this is not really what I do. I'm a voice coach by training.

Adultery is multifaceted, he said. It's shapeless but at the same time has a rudimentary figure, like a snowflake; an abundance of clichés surround it and yet it's unique, an entity different each time. Over the window in his bedroom was a grate secured with a large padlock. The sun came through the grate and then the embroidered curtains he brought back from Spain, spreading a lattice across her body that he traced with his fingers, from her belly—with its cesarean scar—to her chin.

There was the inelegance of it, too, of course, and the requisite lies that must be told, and the foolishness they felt when alone: his feeling of desertion when she was up at her house along the river. He went down near the water, to walk the length of Riverside Park, to breathe the creosote and salt air, and to look at the edge of the Palisades beyond the bridge.

The superstructure that held the subway where it emerged from the tunnel at Broadway and 125th Street. The brutal way the trains heaved to a stop, out of sight but not out of earshot—the clandestine sensation of secreting some part of his life away.

They made love in his apartment most afternoons, one way or another, during lunch.

•

I don't care about this job. I'm a part-timer. I'm not obligated to this career, he said.

We provide fine insurance for religious institutions under the umbrella, but otherwise we're just another business; we weigh the risk factors—and she stopped herself here because it was easy, she found, to fall into a mindless prattle about the nature of the insurance business, about the ways risks were covered. This subject, along with the embroidered curtains, made her think of the time in Spain, with her husband, when they had gone up onto the mesa for dinner with a British couple, a man who worked for Lloyd's of London. She remembered something seminal about that night; they had felt so young, so fresh, so keenly American. They drank a punch made of Pimm's and talked about life. Then there had been—and here she was somewhat fuzzy on the details—an insinuation about group sex? A hint at some form of experimentation? It was never clear. They'd excused themselves, gone to the car, driven down the road into Carboneras, laughing and excited, cutting straight through the town. The street busy, jammed with people, she had sensed the carrying of a secret agreement, of something deep and unspoken.

The night when the circumstances were correct—her daughter was on a sleepover with a friend, her husband away on business—they took a cab through the park to the East Side for dinner, roaring through the trees, the redolent smell of the earth, passing the old horse stables, to emerge into a larger order, the stateliness of Park Avenue.

The rattle of the emerging subway, salsa music from gypsy cabs—if he listened, when she woke him to make love again, he heard these sounds coalesce and deteriorate into nothingness: the quaint, paradoxical dynamic of knowing and not knowing. She'd become acutely aware of this sensation much later, when she moved back to the city and was living near Park Avenue, looking down at the traffic.

The great sorrow of being part of the overall tradition, for lack of a better phrase: knowing that Chekhov had it right. They read "The Lady with the Pet Dog" together, in the grass in the park, lying on a blanket, while across the street, near Grant's Tomb, a boy lifted a pit bull up by a stick to strengthen its jaw.

I'd come to Lincoln Center some night, he said, when you're with your husband, and watch you two listening to the symphony. I'd meet you at the fountain during the intermission and we'd steal away.

No, we'd meet just as we're meeting now. Except it would go on forever. The story would end and then it would just keep going, the way this one does. That's what it's about. It would keep going onward, like the light from a star. We know they're not going to find a way out, around it, and we know that they're just going to continue until it ends.

•

But it doesn't end, he said. He was on his back with his hand behind his head and the sun coming down through the bristle of his whiskers.

Around the edge of her voice when she was tense, or anxious, came the tightness of her Midwestern upbringing; she spoke one afternoon about her daughter. She's, well, how should I say this? She's kind of a troubled teenage kid. Maybe not much different than most. A little on the edge. *Troubled* is the only word I can find for it. I try never to say it because to say it is to make it so. But saying it to you seems safe enough.

The point where lust and love meet, where one ends and the other begins: the innate sincerity buried in the act of betrayal. The way it revealed the vestiges of her home to her, so that upon her return she saw everything, the pebbles in the driveway a buttermilk color, the old shingles smeared with moss, the clapboards lifting away from their nails, the yard wide and grand all the way down to the water's edge, the light in her daughter's room through the curtains . . .

Dressing in the morning, snapping and adjusting undergarments, examining herself in the mirror with one hand on her belly, like Napoleon, lifting her skirt up her over her thighs, the single spritz of perfume around her belt line, all in the pale predawn light. With her mug of coffee at the kitchen sink, craning a bit to see if the traffic was heavy on the bridge: a chain of moving lights. She would cross it in a few minutes and go to the platform and wait, feeling a small soft pulse in her groin.

They stood together on the grating over the East River Drive, in the whoosh of updraft, and engaged in a long kiss while beside them the river gathered the last light of the Manhattan day. The kiss brought them as close to floating, as close to flying, as they'd ever get, and proved to be the most memorable moment, one that would remain with her for the rest of her life: the tangle of her hair around his face and lips, the touch of his fingers near the waistband of her skirt, while the cars passed beneath.

Using the excuse of work obligation, she came in on a Sunday, met him in the doorway of his building, and they walked to a service together. The reverend's voice boomed past the microphone, reverberating hard against the stone, speaking about the elegance of grace, about the manner of forgiveness and the nature of redemption. He quoted from the book of Job:

> *The squares of the town forget them;*
> *their name is no longer remembered;*
> *so wickedness is broken like a tree.*

On top of the flat pleats of her tweed skirt, tight against her spreading thighs, their hands rested, clasped firmly.

One year, from start to finish, the affair bent in a great arch, the first hints of lust building into the long lovemaking sessions at the apartment, twisting into the thick helix of obligation, the secretiveness of talk.

I want you to see the house, she said. I want you to know where I live, to get an idea. I want you to know a little bit about my life the way I know about yours. I'd like you to see my daughter. I want to kiss you on the riverbank, to implicate you into my existence . . .

He rented a car, an old blue Ford—the kind of car a priest might drive—and drove across the bridge, turning up to the parkway as she had directed, exiting and following the river, crossing the town to her house, which stood up a drive—complacent-looking, just as she had described it, with its white clapboard and the lawn behind it stretching down to the water. He drove to the end of the road, to the park she had mentioned, and turned around and went past the house again. In his ribs was the clench of sadness. There was a light on in the upstairs window, behind a gauze of cotton, soft and yellowish. Her bedroom, he knew, was in the back and out of sight, facing the water.

He waited in the coffee shop for darkness to arrive, and emerged back into a soft fall evening. This time the house was silent and dark, and the car in the driveway was gone.

·

At the lookout off the Palisades Parkway, in her car, the lights of the Bronx a Milky Way of stars quivering in the Indian summer heat: Every year a kid falls from the Palisades here, she said, or leaps. I've talked to my daughter . . . *mouths kissing* . . . about it, about the dangers . . . *kissing, parting* . . . there is a reasonableness in her, there is something that still listens . . .

As she left her office, the thin black skirt she wore was overcharged with static. She sprayed it and felt it lift away, but by the time she was back on the street it was recharged, clinging in wavelets to her thighs, riding along her crotch, sliding up with each step as she climbed the stairs to his apartment, where, in the wintry afternoon light, she stood before him and marched, letting the hem rise up and up her thighs until he was on his knees, clutching her waistband by the elastic.

There was the disrobing, the unveiling, the sublime exposure. The sunlight was low and cold; a bitter wind came in across Riverside. The heat in the pipes lurched and thumped, and from the steam valve there came a sputter, the sound of lips parting. He opened the window and she thought of her own house, leaking heat, the old plaster cold to the touch. It was that simple, in some ways, the wonder of the affair, the sense of lines that were drawn and redrawn: to have demarcations so clear and perfect, like lines on a map, not the regions and countries but the everlasting longitudes and latitudes; that part she retained when all else was gone.

·

He's rather serious, she told a friend. Of course he has to be a bit serious, because he is studying theology. He speaks Hebrew and some Aramaic and is studying the Psalms . . . but he's funny, and not too serious, really, and you wouldn't know from meeting him that he's going to be a man of the cloth.

He's funny, she told another friend. He's lighthearted, with this nasal twang of a voice that somehow gets to me, you know, and he can turn phrases and do things that get inside me and make me feel alive.

The shame she felt came from the truth: she had been fucked and was fucking. The carnality of the affair was brutal and the main point. She wore the skirt again, electrified by the dry winter air, and let the static build as she walked along his street.

When you argue about your own story, she explained, well, that's the end of things. As soon as we started to argue about our story, things fell apart for us.

When they tried to get God in, when he mentioned the idea of God nudging them together, the narrative, she would later think, immediately became banal and meek, rooted in the world. It was near the end. On a clear spring day the promenade urged them south. Beneath the wall that ran along Riverside Drive a man lay asleep on an old, splintered bench, his fat belly spilling from green work pants, a newspaper folded over his

face. On the next bench sat another man wearing thick head-
phones, moving his head placidly in small rotations, as if
working out an eternal kink in his neck. There was something
unsettling about his deep absorption in music that could not be
heard and that would never be heard.

They went down toward the river, cutting off the promenade
along a thin dusty path through the weeds. He let her go a few
yards ahead so he could watch her hips shifting beneath her
skirt, the movement of her rear against the silk fabric, light- and
dark-blue daisy-shaped flowers. There was that helplessness in
her movement—from her pumps on the unsteady ground—that
he enjoyed, a sense that she might tumble at any moment, and
she did, twisting sideways to the right with a small grunt, and
falling into the weeds.

The bone was broken—a spiral fracture—just above her ankle.
With her arm around his shoulder, and his arm around hers,
they hobbled up the path, along the promenade, to Riverside
Drive, where they hailed a cab and went all the way up to
Columbia Presbyterian Hospital.

In his apartment—cool with blue twilight—she lay on his bed
while he ran his fingers along the soft cotton gauze, against the
fiberglass, that spot where the two met. He'd remember that
forever. His finger going up and in against the warmth of her
foot, slipping as far as it would go.

·

On the way to the car, I was stepping off the curb and twisted it and the bone bore the brunt, she explained to her husband. I got a cab to this hospital and then went back to get my bag from the car. The story felt frail and feeble, like old lace; it had the gaping open spaces you'd expect, although it was made carefully, with consideration of all the angles. He chose to believe it. He let his compassion—his duty as a good husband—slip like mortar between the cracks. Much later he'd examine his foolishness and think: I was as complicit as she was in that story, driving in to pick her up, finding her standing up, leaning against the car.

A fetid, oily smell emerged from beneath the cast: sweat, dead skin, and dirt. Afternoons, she lay on a divan in the back room and read Tolstoy.

The way bone heals, calcifying and thickening and becoming stronger. The knob of new bone you can feel against the skin. The elation of the cast being removed, the saw touching the skin but not cutting, the sudden sensation of freedom.

Summer was deep and warm. Behind them the office building, with its reflective glass, collected and cubed the vista. The great terminus of parting; the deep, elegiac tragedy of it. The upstate reservoirs had been depleted by the heat wave, their dirty skirts powdered with dried algae and muck. Spray caps were attached to the fireplugs, unleashing thin, tight streams, until the kids removed the caps with lug wrenches. The dry silence of a late Friday in early July. Broadway, visible from the corner, was strangely empty.

*

Never mutual, the fact that one must suffer more than the other, however preordained, seemed startling. Ginkgo nuts fell early from trees along Claremont Avenue—the drought had urged the season forward—and a man collected them in a cloth sack, working slowly in the heat, plucking them up one at a time.

Her explanation was stilted: First she talked about her marriage and her daughter and the fact that she was not willing to give these things up, to let them go, and then, fumbling for something more specific, she said, I went last night to check my daughter, and she was uncovered and sleeping facedown and I looked at her back, the bones of her back, and they were, well, they reminded me of the bones of a sardine. You could chew and swallow them and not even notice.

I believed it myself when I told him that, she said to a friend.

To go back to Chekhov: the torment of it, the way it was rooted in place—the hot winds of Yalta, the wintry streets of Moscow. In her case it was the long stretch of riverfront at the end of the yard at home: then the gray spans of the bridge, with the city, down to the right, stretched lengthwise into the summer haze.

The potential was there for a long time: He'd show up in her town, unexpectedly, standing with his hands stuffed deep into his pockets, or at Lincoln Center, as he had proposed, during intermission, the next tier down, spotted through the glass railing, looking, searching.

Much later, she'd hold specific memories of it: the clandestine ventures out into the night; the way the grid of north-south streets seemed to contain them, walking hand in hand down Columbus in the fall, dressed in sweaters, relishing the itch of the wool. A man had been selling cashmere scarves from a sheet of cardboard near the Plaza Hotel. He'd bought one and lifted it gently around her neck.

Weirdly enough, I lied and told him my daughter was sixteen, and troubled, she admitted to a friend. I added four years to my own daughter's life and didn't know why I was doing it at the time.

There was deliberation at the deepest level, even in the falling away, the parting, the bitterness. There was an inelegance. No matter how fanciful and wild, no matter how impulsive, in retrospect it had stood within the fact of the marriage itself. Still, she beheld a certain dignity in the exactitudes: the smell of cut flowers at a bodega, rubber bands bright red around their stems; the dusky light off Broadway on summer afternoons; the heavy wall along Riverside Park, cool against their calves, as they sat holding hands during lunch, turning now and then to glance down through the trees to the river, which was broken up into shards, a deep blue against the green.

Facts Toward Understanding the Spontaneous Human Combustion of Errol McGee

The Fire

A violet rashlike spume of vapors circumnavigated his ankles and then spread over his shins—freckled, smeared with age spots—until, reaching the conflagration point, he burst into a senseless mass of orange flame. Presumably he didn't writhe or squirm because by the time the fire hit (or perhaps before) he was unconscious. The position of his chair indicates that he probably had his heels up on the windowsill. Staring off at the lake with his feet up, the bottle tucked in his crotch, he was resting in a wicker chair, which of course remained miraculously unscorched. People found the things that weren't burned astonishing: the chair, the curtains, the porch, the cottage itself. Above his skull, on the ceiling over the chair, a large blister of seared paint had formed. The first fireman on the scene couldn't help himself. He popped it with the tip of his ax.

The Skull

There's the undeniable physical reality of the evidence: the skull, cleaned of flesh, resting on the green seat cushion; window curtains—blue swirls of highly flammable Dacron—twisting in the lake breeze, perfectly intact after the conflagration, not even a singe except where, years ago, McGee's ex-wife had let the iron rest a little too long. Again, the ceiling blister, so obviously the result of aggressive heat, but still only a blister. (Admittedly, the ceiling tiles had some asbestos fibers to retard fire, but not enough to prevent flames from driving through to ignite the furring strips and up into the dry-baked rafters. Presumably, a fire that was hot enough to carbonize bone—with the weird exception of the skull—would be enough to ignite a structure. Too neat, the fireman thought, seeing it. Too damn tidy.)

General Conditions

Full S.H.C. events leave nothing but a very faint trace of ash and a shadow of the deceased, if even that, and in rare cases a lamina of glass coating the object upon which the victim (for lack of a better way to put it) stood, sat, or reclined. Most often the victim is seated with some view or vista at hand: a lakeside or seashore or the broad expanse of some grand river, and in rare cases a wide field, or a savanna, and in even rarer cases no view at all except a television screen, in which instance the device is invariably implicated as the cause—or spark—of the event: blame placed willy-nilly, in the grope for an explanation, squarely on the shoulders of the boob tube (as it was called) and its ability to create flashes of stupid heat, produced out of the dull vagaries of mind-numb sitting when—the theory goes—all deep thoughts are purged to leave a void that is quickly filled with a flux of bodily processes: regiments of cells rebelling against a vegetative state and going haywire as they break into a symbiotic self-eating festival. A somewhat absurd reaction, admittedly, but perhaps justified, depending on the view.

Udall's Natural Hair Ointment

McGee had steely gray hair combed neatly back and held to his scalp with a lacquer of Udall's Natural Hair Ointment, vintage 1945, of which there were large quantities found in the cottage medicine cabinet and under the bathroom sink, sixty bottles in all, which led to one early theory that some of this tonic had saturated his skin and, in turn, his cell walls, and somehow, when he lit a cigarette (another key bit of evidence: a soft pack of Winstons, half gone, and a box of kitchen matches on the windowsill), sparked a violent combustion.

Before he fell into the bottle in a big way, McGee had been obsessive about his bodily care, although he had shunned modern products such as deodorant sticks for his own methods: that is, sprinkling his armpits with bay rum. In general, he was a man of outmoded customs: toothpicks for tooth cleaning; links to secure the cuffs; bandanas, and later fine linen handkerchiefs, folded neatly into the front pocket and occasionally taken out for a good, loud nose blow. McGee was a virtuosic nose blower, and his colleagues from his early days at the mill, those still alive, say he blew loud enough to be heard over the roar of the press drums and even the final rollers. One dubious theory has it that intense pressure in the nasal cavities can somehow induce spontaneous combustion.

The American Dream

Back when he was the head of Mear Paper, a firm that produced more wire-bound notebooks, check pads, carbon backing sheets, lined and unlined twenty-pound bond than any mill west of Maine, he used to say: It ain't nothing to making goddamn paper. Find a few trees, chop 'em down, mash 'em up, add water. In just a few years he went from general mill hand to welder, to electrician, to manager, to owner and president.

Eventually, the large pond that settled to the west of the main plant and the plume of dioxins that leached into the aquifer were blamed for the cancer cluster that stretched in a tongue shape from Drake Street—old row housing originally built when the wax paper facility was erected in the early for- ties—to the end of Crane Avenue, where it ended abruptly at the location of McGee's elegant Queen Anne–style home. His fall seemed mythic to those who saw him in his later years, dressed in his old mill overalls, stained black along the hip where his tool belt had worn a greasy spot, staggering outside of Hawks near the railroad station. Hawks, your bottom-end drunk bar and hobo hangout set as close to the double set of tracks—Chicago–Detroit, Detroit–Chicago—as it could get; Hawks, not much more than a tar paper shack with the obliga- tory single neon sign in the window, a pale pink outline of a cocktail glass sputtering epileptically.

The War in Vietnam

As one theory goes: McGee was fascinated by the protest immolation of monks in Vietnam, and had once been overheard saying he could understand the notions that get behind a man when he douses himself with gas to make a point. Inside his mill locker—kept as a gesture of solidarity with his employees—he had taped a magazine photo of Thich Quang Duc being consumed by flames. He studied it occasionally and marveled at the discipline of the monk in relation to the hungry disorder of the fire itself.

He talked sometimes of napalm: In retrospect it seems fit, to those who speculate on the cause of his S.H.C., to note that his son, Haze, was killed by the arrant use of this weapon/ product in that war, a fact laying a bit of credence to the theory that McGee's combustion was a sympathetic reaction, albeit delayed a few decades, to the news delivered by a soldier one May morning to the Queen Anne house on Crane Avenue. It is not inconceivable—to those who have endured the same kind of grief—that a man, on a hot summer night, reminiscing about his son, would draw up the deep pain of that loss much the way the wick (see "Wick Theory," below) supposedly draws the melted fat, and in doing so might himself become overheated with the fires of melancholy and explode into sorrow-fueled flames.

Gloria

Some say McGee had a lover, a Chicago showgirl/call girl named Gloria who with his help came up on the New York Central and settled into the Delvic Hotel downtown. His old friend Marlin Duke recalls hearing him mumble something about his love flame, or having to attend to his love flame.

Perhaps in the white heat of memory, conjuring up the smooth skin of her forearms, the glossy smooth plain of flesh at the base of her spine, the husky elocutions of her smoky voice,

or more specifically the way she had stood amid the long, slant-
ing sun shafts in Union Station one fall afternoon, clutching her
bag, reaching to adjust the pin that secured her pillbox hat,
McGee had simply drawn too deeply from the well of memory
that evening at the lake, sucked it all eagerly back, so that it
stood in a stasis between his body and mind, in that delicate
tissue, where it had congealed and fermented into a single
spark bright and hot enough to ignite that final, albeit limited,
inferno.

The Great Depression

Temperance workers attributed S.H.C. to drink and found a
neat way to attach their moral/political agenda to the phenome-
non by saying: That's where the drunk burned, lost to the sins
of corn whiskey, hard cider, boot brandy, bourbon, and ripple,
until his body—mercy be to the Lord our host—absorbed too
much of the distillate and burst forth in a fire of Judgment. Up
and down the Dust Bowl countryside, at the bottoms of hopper
cars, in the corners of empty reefers you'd find them, bleached
white, skulls and feet, the relics of the Lord's Judgment left to
remind the living of the necessity for Temperance.

Wick Theory

In one controlled experiment a sedated pig was wound in cotton
gauze—wrapped tight, swaddled like a newborn—and then set
ablaze to prove the "wick effect." The theory: The fire, fed by
the bubbling fat as flames wicked through the cotton, would
sustain itself in a concentrated form until the fat and bones
were carbonized and the cotton itself burned away and only the

head, falling from the flames, would be left with the proverbial pile of ash and some smoke stains on the laboratory ventilation bib. Throughout the experiment, the subject's snout moved up and down, softly nodding.

Early Flame Experience

Through the smoked goggles the flame looked tight and made small, lip-smacking twists as it touched the metal and then blew out the spark bloom. At an early age, McGee proved himself a brilliant welder and could draw a clean, neat line that tapered out to a beadless end. His relationship with fires in general and flames in particular was a good one, his coworkers said; and after he went to electricians' school in Detroit, he returned to the mill with a deep understanding of spark formation and an assured intuition that allowed him to tinker in high-voltage boxes without shutting the power. It was said he could grab one of the giant fuses barehanded and yank it without a flinch. How these facts connect with the overall mystery of his end remains unclear, although it is often said that beneath any mystery lies another, even deeper one, and some speculate that his abilities around electrical forces and, in turn, the fires they could or might create were connected to the fact that on that summer night, alone in his cottage, he found some neat and tidy final arrangement with the demise he had avoided so easily at a time when his life was moving with such vigor and ease into an ascendancy. So it seems natural to some that all of the avoided fires—the curse of any electrician—would finally come back to haunt him in one singular burst, and in so doing provide his decline with a terminal end.

Family

First the divorce from his wife, Angel, after she discovered he was hiding his lover at the Delvic; then the death of his son in the war; and then a few years later, the automobile accident that took his daughter, Grace, on a road north of Gary, Indiana.

The Lake & Cottage

On the evening of his death the water was serene and flat and unusually glossy as dusk hung over the lake. The failing daylight lent it an unusual copper color, so that from his vantage, on the porch, he watched while all that remained of the day poured itself out into the water and then was sucked into an obsidian form surrounded by the silhouettes of trees and, above those, a blue-black sky with stars peeking through—all this on an evening when the first hints of fall entered the air. (No one can say exactly why, but it seems important that it was a mild evening, not too hot, not too cold, and that the fire that consumed him could not be attributed, say, to one of the long hot spells that plagued the state with blazes that summer.) His cottage had degenerated from pristine, freshly painted each year, to shabby and run-down, with scales of lead flakes coming off the clapboards and a rank odor emerging from beneath the porch. The pavestones on the steps down to the beach had crumbled like blue cheese, and the dock, left out to freeze in the ice over the years, lurched vulgarly to one side.

Variants

Perhaps it helps to imagine those recently discovered variants of lightning that appear between sky and space along the upper reaches of thunderheads: red sprites, mushrooming elves, electric (smoke) rings clutching at the sinkhole of space.

Perhaps it helps to imagine the small sparks of current between the cell walls, bunching up into the endoplasmic reticulum, congealing in the ribosome; those tight nuggets of life until, swarming like killer bees, certain charges cohere, gather heat, and then—well, then there is nothing but raw resistance and flame. Perhaps it is simply useful to remind oneself that there are still unseen mysteries at hand.

Square Dancing

Even when he was president of Mear Paper, riding shotgun in his modified Checker with its chrome sideboards, wet bar, and flashy leather backseats, he'd order his chauffeur to stop at the VFW hall so he could watch the Friday square dance called by Burt Michigan Wolverine, whose barking voice created intricate patterns as partners linked arms and rotated in that effortless yet demanding tension when there is just enough lust (and love) between pairs to make their temporary partings seem lonely and tragic until their reunifications at the end.

Potentially Related Strange Phenomena

Barns catching fire—on hot summer afternoons—out of the blue and for no apparent reason; a person disappearing in the dead of night, leaving only a pile of blankets on the bed and an ash-stenciled outline of his or her last sleeping formation; war hoots along the border of Kansas; the lonely, dim-throated voice of Riding Thunder, or Kit Carson, seeping into the radio static.

Additional Theories: The Spiral Notebook

Word was McGee had a fascination with the idea of the spiral notebook, and even claimed that he had invented the product himself. He expressed admiration for the curl of wire embracing the punched holes, drawing the pages into a tight alliance. One old-timer remembers seeing him in the break room during his electrician days, fiddling with wire, twisting it around a dowel. Only through stubborn will is it possible to fit his obsession with the spiral notebook into the manner in which he died that evening at the lake, and in doing so one has to turn to a grand theory that includes the ideas of symmetry and of the spiral in relation to the stress—and heat and friction—certain bond papers produce when a sheet is torn away. But that is a stretch.

Additional Theories: Dynamite

In order to make room for the proposed civic center, a crew came up from Chicago and examined the Delvic's structure and set packets of explosives in strategic spots and wired them all together. There was something hopeful in their bright orange hard hats and the casual manner with which they handled the deadly materials. They spent an inordinate amount of time locating and packing the mythic main beam—that singular elemental piece of iron that acted as the crux for the entire superstructure. They stood in the street with surveying tripods and figured the angles and odds and estimated the rate of fall and the potential width of the dust ball that would come out of the mass like a giant furry beast. The fat ornate facade of the hotel—which had at one time lent the town an optimistic sense of grandeur and hope, with its curly cues of rococo molding and Louis Sullivan–inspired terra-cotta, and its gargoyles frog-like and malformed, hunched in the top corners and visible only at twilight when the sun spread across the heavens—stood even after the blast, while the skeletal innards slid down in slow motion, the way a warm wedding cake might melt (all this transpiring in a few seconds of dust-bloom wonder); but if you looked closely—people say, people who were there—you could see the facade heaving, radiating hairline fractures as it struggled against its forthcoming demise. Other onlookers swear they didn't see a thing.

Gloria

Some say McGee was in the audience on Bronson Street, sitting in the bleachers with the rest of the crowd, when the signal was given and the wired packets exploded and the building held still for a dignified moment, emitting small puffs of smoke. Some town folk claim that Gloria waved to him—her hand, in a white glove, mistaken for one of the many pigeons leaving their roosts at the last moment. She had hidden herself in a storage closet, amid galvanized buckets and the stagnant smell of wet mop heads and pink floor soap, emerging into the empty hallway only when the building was silent and the evacuation team was gone. (Common assumption is that she hid herself away with the expectation that McGee would stop the explosions and rescue her; others say she was mentally ill and paranoid and couldn't imagine herself living anywhere else. Most agree that McGee thought she was safely out of the building.)

The fire marshal says that when they dynamited the Donavon Hotel in Chicago—previous home to an assortment of vagabonds and junkies, a remnant of the great flophouse culture of the Depression—they found the bodies of three men dressed in old tuxedos and the top hats of industrialists, with cigars still clenched in their teeth and cards in their hands. One, he says, had a pretty good hand, a full house, and seemed to be smiling, as if in that final moment of brain spark he had found deep pleasure not only in the good luck of his draw but also in meeting a benevolent grace-giving God who could at once provide justice and allow the persistence of deeper mysteries, the things that went beyond perhaps even His (God's) own wide providence during yet another troubled period in American history. (See "The Great Depression," above.)

The Botch

The idea is to tap into the old traditions, guns waving, eyes behind balaclavas—just one more bank heist breaking the tedium of an Ohio afternoon, leaving nothing but bewilderment, the kind you'd expect from corn-fed farm folks, one or two Mennonites, along with the requisite towheaded kid in overalls, his shoulders slumped from hauling seed bags; maybe a mother, one of those dry-mouth screamers, unleashing a dog-whistle cry (From a face begging to be pistol-whipped, Carson cut in) with that lonely look that comes from long, empty hours mashing up vegetables and boiling bottles on the stove, spoon-feeding the baby in a house amid the dead fields. She'll go from that dog-whistle scream to cold fear to a kind of longing in a matter of a minute, gathering hope from the barrel of a gun, that dark rictus behind which the bore grooves lie ready to spin a bullet to a perfect stability, until it arrives to release her from the obligations of her life, so to speak. The idea being that her life, seeing that gun, hearing the shouts, for a startling moment will become strangely meaningful. Idea is to stand coolly, legs apart for balance, moving the gun from the farm-boy kid to the farm wife to the Old Order Mennonite, slowly enough to offer each of them a chance to have the aforementioned sensation, Donnie explained, pausing for a moment to suck on his cigar, glancing around our hideout, an old blacksmith shed about twenty miles outside Gallipolis, nothing inside but an old forge, stone cold, with taut, dried-out bellows, a few rickety chairs, an old table nicked and scarred from years of horseshoe pounding, and a dusty window giving a view of the road and a field of dead corn. Idea is to know ahead of time—because it's pretty much preordained—that the security codger will be sitting on a stool near the front door, ready to put up some kind of fight, Donnie said, slapping the forge with the side of his palm, leaning down to gaze out the window while we stood around and waited for him to continue.

Before we left that day we conducted a dry run of commands and gestures, scuffing through charcoal dust in the dreary afternoon light, drawing together into a huddle formation, arms over shoulders, trying to establish a sense of camaraderie, a communal intent, an esprit de corps so tight and consuming that it would—when the time came—allow for an intuitive coordination of gestures, the kind of cohesion of action that comes from knowing a role by heart, pure muscle memory and nothing else, so that when we were done with the heist and making our getaway, we'd carry only physical sensations— twitches, cold gun metal, a grimace. Nothing useful for an interrogator to piece together. No dots to connect, Donnie said. No consistency in the story from one man to the next. Again, the idea would be to make sure we factored in the old codger and the solitude his face might contain, having, most likely, lived a widower's life the past five years or so (All widowers, these bank guards in Ohio, Carson said). One must factor in a no-nonsense attitude on his part, forged in confrontations with the likes of Dillinger. If not top guys, then at least bootleggers making the West Virginia–Cleveland run. Not so much the Capone gang per se, although Capone's shadow had loomed all the way down into these parts, but more likely bit players with nothing to lose. Most likely the codger had had at least one genuine run-in with a stickup artist over the course of a long career in these parts. Guys like Jim Molloy and Stark Wallhouse—running product down from Pittsburgh, speaking in their snappy, big-city vernacular, riding roughshod over the law—have left a bitter taste in the mouths of retired cops all over the state. Idea will be to show a bit of panache in the way we handle things, so that the old codger and the other victims sense that the outcome is simply out of their hands and follow the easiest course, moving as directed, moving to the right-hand side of the room (always the right) while in the back the bagman collects the money. Idea being not to spook, but to keep the fear level steady and cool. Closing the blinds, if necessary, and trusting in the wider dynamic. Idea is to entrust the job not to the hands of some kind of fate, Donnie explained, relighting his cigar, rolling the tip in the flame, taking a couple of deep draws, sucking hard, trying to get the smoke from one end to the other. But rather to tap into the rubbery nature of all that cash, eager to be relieved of the restrictions of the bank. The idea being that most good folks will side with the money and, in turn, with us. After so many years in the desolate countryside—in particular the Mennonite-slash-Amish, tired of all that harness adjusting, the hard clop of shoe iron on modern roads, the wheel hoops sparking the pavement, not to mention sunup-to-sundown toil, trying to make ends meet without most of the

modern conveniences—they will side with the monetary release
and, as a result, secretly root for our success while recognizing,
I might add, he said, taking another deep puff, the ethos of our
work and the fact that we're Robin Hoods of a sort, doing our
best to free the money from its reluctant association with the
bank and the big syndicate empires of speculation. Idea is to
assure them—through the stateliness of our behavior—that the
money will land in the hands of men who have suffered indi-
rectly from the Great Depression years, at the hands of parents
who had scrimped and scraped, rode the rails (my old man),
gone door to door begging meals (my old man), sold apples on
the streets (Carson's old man), ran backwoods stills down in
Clark County (Donnie's old man), lived hand to mouth by their
wits, only to come out of those years hardened in a smithy of
desperation, the skin tight around their jaws (my father), ready
to beat thriftiness into their sons (all of our fathers). Suffering
while the syndicate men hooked their thumbs into their vests,
spread their fingers across their fat bellies, and retreated to their
oak-paneled dens to ride out the storm. Idea is to take advantage of the fact that the heist itself will cause most of the folks
in the bank to look back at a time when those of our ilk were
heroes while we, for our part, make a getaway into the future,
tearing out of town with a flamboyant wildness that comes
from knowing—after belt whippings, after knuckle rapping,
after verbal berating—that what we have in hand is rightly ours,
for keeps.

The flex of time against unmitigated factors. The intrusion of
the unknown into the idea of the heist in such a way that you
cannot possibly attribute the botch that transpired to a failure

of planning. It came with the folks who were there from the start, not only the old security codger—named Ed, Earl, or Ike—but also those in line, including the Old Order Mennonite who turned at Donnie's commands to present placid eyes and a grim mouth. He held the look of a man who was obligated to only one commander. A few of the farmer types stayed put until they saw the gun barrel. Then the line bowed—a small tow-headed boy, two women who were just about to shriek—until Donnie went up to the Mennonite and put the gun close in, not touching but close enough to give him something to really think about. (And the man did think. You could see it in his pale, serene gaze. In the way he lifted his shoulders slightly. He had that neat, tidy composure that came from the grace of God, I thought at the window, glancing out at the street and then back inside, trying to keep my head clear, to see both sides of the coin, so to speak.) Donnie moved close and a tension formed. Meanwhile, in the back, Carson was working the bagman routine, hefting his tommy gun, scaring up some cash. In those first few moments everything unfolded. The security codger was on his side, on the floor. (We'd pistol-whipped him first, taking him by surprise and from behind, sending him down to the floor for a few kicks, his gun pinwheeling away. He was there for a reason, we knew, and that reason was if not to resist then to look startled and frail, to make us feel a bit more of the guilt that came from our obligations; just as the small kid, the towheaded one, was there to remind us that we had a duty to avoid the botch, to make things run smoothly, if possible, and to keep order.) But the Old Order Mennonite stood firm and absorbed the orders—Donnie was barking hard at him, his neck straining—while the ladies cried, tipping their heads back slightly, exposing the napes of their necks, making birdlike motions, as if waiting to be fed, while back behind the counters Carson bustled. Everything was smooth from my vantage. Everything was moving neatly along the general plan, even the Old Order Mennonite, who was a factor already factored in. Bags were being filled up, and Carson's talent for getting action out of the tip of his gun, of turning fear into motion, was in full play. He rocked the gun against his hip and worked it slowly in relation to his thin, lean, whiplash Okie frame, carrying himself with a formality, a politeness that was tight to his jaw. Just hearing the snap in his voice you know that everything sluiced down into a particular moment, a void of air where money slipped into those bags. The tart tension of those bags! The feeling in the air of transaction! Time fluxed around a point in space near Carson. It bent around the fear and fluxed smoothly around the Old Order Mennonite (or Old Order Amish), pouring around him as he held his ground, his spit-shined shoes tight to the floor.

Idea was to glance out at the view—the clean vista of Third Avenue to the west, and Cedar Street to the east—and then inside for a few seconds before glancing out again, finding the right balance and speed to hold both (inside and outside) in mind at the same time; never really taking my eye off the ball, so to speak, and in that manner backing up Donnie and maybe even Carson, who might need me to run back to help with the loot. Idea was to find a groove and to stay in it, not losing the sense that the outside world was inside, too, in a way, and in that manner also—and this defies logic, but then so does a good heist—assure that no one would come wandering in to disrupt the job.

A quick glance back told me Donnie was doing his part, speaking out the side of his mouth—sans cigar—and holding his edge, adjusting himself quickly to the scene, making sure he had the upper hand on the Old Order Mennonite, while, in the back, Carson worked his role of bagman, took the counters, whispering his commands to tellers and bank officials in a low voice that drew them close, aching to hear, eager to get it right, and in turn allowed each of them a good look at the tommy gun, which he hefted in a certain way, cradling it against his hips. All in all—I thought—he was the perfect guy for the job and played the role to the hilt, bearing himself in a stately manner under the weight of responsibility that came from being the apex, the guy at the point of transference. Tall and lean, he moved like a movie star, all style, limberly urging folks with small, delicate nudges of the barrel, making improvised gestures, taking what he could as fast as he could, maintaining an absolute cool, speaking with that hayseed politeness, the kind that comes from feeling perpetually outclassed. He rarely lost his cool. When he did, it was usually in the form of a single shot to the head.

In the parlance of the profession she might be called a natural distraction factor. (Cops are an unnatural distraction factor, arriving creaky and stiff-jointed. Cops hobble in fearfully, all leather squeak and handcuff clatter.) A natural distraction factor appears as part of the everyday landscape: a white gull making lovely swooping motions in the sky (the Atlantic City Trust botch) or an unusual calico cat sleeping on the hood of a car (the North Dakota National Bank botch in Fargo), or a kid with a Pretty Boy Floyd face drinking a soda pop (the Fresno Botch/Massacre). Natural distraction factors draw the player—usually the door guy—away momentarily from the strict mechanics of the heist, creating not only a few beats of stark distraction but also a wider sense of perspective, reorienting the mind so that the player must, when he returns his attention to the job at hand, reconnect with the nature of his obligations in relation to the task. In this case the natural distraction factor appeared across the street, moving carefully, sashaying her hips against a tight red skirt, arms loaded with bags. Her hair was piled in a fantastic beehive of blond over her pale forehead as she stumbled in her high heels, just off balance enough to lend her an alluring vulnerability. She moved through attractive obliviousness as she struggled against her burdens, swinging those hips in easy gyrations.

Idea was to avoid the following:

The silent-alarm botch, in which case some trigger-happy teller takes pleasure in knowing that a posse of jazzed-up cops is roaring through the streets, eager to get to the scene but keeping the sirens off and trying to avoid wheel screeches, all because he fingered the button at the first sign of a stickup.

The mix-up botch, in which preplanned roles become fused so that, say, the bagman, in the head of the job, finds it necessary to help with the herding, and in so doing opens up, as it were, a force vacuum leading (perhaps) to a silent-alarm trigger botch, and/or:

A heroic fallacy botch, in which one soul stands firm, gathering strength of will from some deeper source—a profound latent rage, perhaps, formed from an overly dramatic sense of fairness—and, seeing the gun muzzle, staring deep into the heart of the bore, feels compelled to side with the idea of authority and thus internalizes the onus of the crime—as he sees it—to the point of active rage, which in turn gives him the strength to stand firm and to resist barked orders. (In a non-botch scenario the hero's vision is lost when he's shot or pistol-whipped. In the nonbotch the intuitive abilities—or the connection to some higher law—is short-circuited by a flush of fear. In the nonbotch scenario the hero lifts his heels from the floor or has an annoying tic: One way or another, all good intent and God connections—in the nonbotch setup—fade when his brainpan is shattered, and he then slumps off with the rest of the customers.) Let it be noted that the botch situation can only, in retrospect, be fully understood in relation to the nonbotch possibilities. Therefore, there is a deeply sentimental aspect to the whole matter. Nothing is sadder than the examination of a crime gone awry. Insofar as these things go, a non-botch scenario (resistant-hero type is shot in the nick of time) can shift to a botch (gunshots alert passerby, or create uncontrollable chaos situation in which the disorder supersedes the ability to forcefully instill order) on a dime. So the idea is to play the two sides against each other to create a harmony between the two potentials. Idea is to avoid second-guessing and to maintain focus on the job at hand: getting the money and fleeing the bank, hooting and hollering in jubilation at a fate avoided, lead-footing it out of town and into the spectacular monotony of the open road.

When I turned from the window that afternoon, after watching the woman with those bags—those ankle-hobbling high heels! the instability of her gait! the afternoon sky firm against the brick facades!—I strained to reorient myself to the heist. But my attention was snagged on that beautiful vision in the street. This led to a classic error. Let me say here that I'll never admit, as some might, to a split in my attention. What transpired was the opposite, actually. The effort that it took to cast the natural distraction factor away (and I did cast her away!) served to sharpen the acuteness of my attention when I swung my gaze back to the interior, and I locked with too much intensity on the resistant factor: the Old School Mennonite refusing Donnie's orders, holding his hands out not with his palms up, but rather with his palms down, lifting them up and down in defiance, as if he were trying to shoo something away. At that moment my obligation—working hard to unsnag myself from the vision in the street—was to stay steady and calm. The idea was to keep cool. But instead I only saw the Old Order Mennonite. I fixed on him and he felt me looking and turned to me and presented his face: lean, long, gaunt around the chin, with a bristle of beard and agate eyes, cold and stony, set beneath busy black brows, above which were deep furrows leading up to a knobby forehead that drove itself into the heavy felt of his black hat. The look he shot me was on equal terms with mine—hard, ruthless, and blunt.

Idea is to push the botch as far it can go, to rally the chaos into an escapable situation, to arrange the disorder into itself, to affirm the oft-repeated phrase—by Carson, mostly—that a good botch ends not with a bang, but with the whisper of shoe leather on pavement. So when Donnie shot the Old Order Mennonite, I shot him at exactly the same time. Then all hell broke loose. One of the tellers in the back began to break away, running forward, and Carson tagged him one in the back of the head. Another dashed to the side—pure panic, no motive, no real intent—and I unleashed one in her direction. Needless to say, the bullets flew. Nothing but the roar and saltpeter in the air and the echoes in the high reaches as we drove the madness into shape and were left with nothing but bags of cash—the two of us—and a persistent ringing in our ears.

Back at the forge the idea was to do a point-by-point analysis and to tweeze apart the boiling chaos, the plumes of blood, the rattle of the tommy gun until it jammed, the inaudible pleas that had draped around us, unheard in the roar. Idea was to find the exact point at which the potential for a botch (hidden in that stalemate between the Old Order Mennonite and Donnie) was somehow nudged over into a genuine bloodbath. Idea was to put aside the residual urgency of the aftermath—the gunmetal tartness on the tongue, the old iron stench of the forge, our sweat-caked shirts—and find something instructive in the mess, the educational moment, so to speak. Otherwise, it was just one more smear of carnage on the floor of one more Ohio bank. Otherwise, it was simply three men going into a rage and spilling blood. To break down the scenario, in retrospect, and to figure out just where the human element had slipped in to ruin what otherwise—up to that moment—had been a purely mechanistic situation: everything moving smoothly along the grand traditions. In most cases—Donnie was saying—you could shave it down to a single moment, freeze-frame it to the precise second just before all hell broke loose, and in doing so locate the blame in one of the following:

A human failing. Nothing too big, nothing tragic, but some

little error on our part. A sudden distraction in the form of a lament for a lost lover, or a stray thought. Some preheist factor, unnoticed before the chain of events began. A second cup of coffee that led to a poorly aimed shot, or a jittery trigger finger. (Good aim requires at least one dose of caffeine. Too much caffeine and you're likely to succumb to the urge, so to speak.)

Some impromptu gesture, Ohio-related. Some improvised response to a gesture on the part of one of the customers—throwing the plan off for a fraction of a second.

We drew a blank that night, with the rain drumming down on the tin roof of the forge. We simply could not find the exact cause. Both of us had shot the Old Order Mennonite, we agreed, at about the same instant, arriving at a mutual conclusion and acting on our instincts in the same manner, and that seemed enough to justify what we did and to set it aside as the actual cause of the botch. We'd drawn from the same visual cues and responded to the best of our abilities swiftly and without too much thought.

In the end—after a lot of mulling, a lot of cigar smoke and pondering—we agreed that the botch might've been caused by some outside factor. Just one of those things. Just another afternoon heist gone bad. We shook hands and gave the forge one last slap for good luck and stepped out into the rain and went our separate ways: Carson headed north toward home; Donnie headed south to Florida; I drove west, staring hard through the swap of the wiper blades, shaking myself awake, doing my best to fend off the desire—and it was a strong one—to return to the bank.

Idea was to go back into the heart of that sad scene, to make an end run around fate by entering into the expectations of the law-enforcement officials (who knew in turn that we in turn knew that they had this expectation), because it was a given that at least one gang member would come stumbling back to the scene of the botch, the brim of his hat pulled low, keeping what he thought was a discreet distance from the scene, lurking in the shadows—so to speak—and holding himself in compliance with the traditions, scapegoating himself to regain some higher sense of order that had been lost in the maelstrom of the botch itself. Just thinking about it was a retreat into vanity. But the impulse was pure and hard. I wanted another shot at the Old Order Mennonite, a chance to fire a few seconds later, deeper into the unfolding drama, to shake loose the image of the woman on the street, who was probably now in bed, I thought, sleeping soundly next to her husband, while in the bowels of the house—nothing less than a big Queen Anne Victorian—a screw rotated, drawing coal into the maw of the fire, keeping them warm and cozy against the chilly night. It was the kind of house a guy like me could only dream about, financed on war loot, backroom deals, and countless bootleg runs. In that house—I imagined, staring out through the rain and dark, trying to keep myself on the road—she slept the deep doze of an innocent. When she woke the next morning she'd go out into her life, sashaying those fine hips, flashing those fine ankles, released from the burden of the truth, never knowing that in the simple act of walking down the street yesterday, she had triggered a dismal botch, a massacre of epic proportions. No: In the morning she'd stretch her arms over her head and yawn, smelling the bacon and coffee downstairs, arching the delicate bones of her shoulders, dreamingly rubbing the sleep from her eyes.

Idea was to stake out the town for days on end, if necessary, watching over cups of coffee in Ralston's diner, knowing full well she'd have to pass that way eventually. Women like that follow strict shopping patterns. A town like Gallipolis has a limited number of retail establishments. The idea was to catch her off guard, to poke the gun into her face and to force her into the car. The idea was to let her know that she had been moving through life the way a fish moves through the water, unable to see the fluid, unable to sort out the larger picture. The idea would be to somehow shift the burden of the botch from my shoulders to her shoulders, heaving it like a duffel loaded with bones of the dead. Then she'd have to raise her arms instinctually—seeing the bag heading her way—and catch it the way a fireman embraces a falling child, bending her knees to ease the weight, lowering herself as far as she could to the ground, staggering under the great weight of the botch itself, catching her balance on the back of her heels.

Oklahoma

Trying to make it look like we were going somewhere, we worked up and down the rows, holding keys in our hands, moving from one car to another in case the guy who monitors the security screens inside the store happened to glance up from his magazine, or his coffee, or his ball game, to catch sight of us. Anyway, no one has ever stopped me, Lester said, and the return policy is sweet because they'll take anything back, no questions asked. You just get the receipt, go inside, find the goods, and then take the stuff to get your money back. In the parking lot that night we had three receipts, including one for a large load of groceries—three hundred dollars' worth. I said, Jesus, this is a lot of food. Lester said, What do you think most people do, starve, you think they don't go in and buy whatever they want? I said, No, I think most kind of save money and then go buy stuff. He said, No, no, they just go and pile it up like that. I said, Okay, okay. He said, You're a dumb shit, for sure. I said, Shut up. He said, Talk more like that, you're out. I said, Sorry. He said, Get looking. I looked, came up with a receipt for a Sony something, called him over, and he said, Bingo, that's it, a big-ticket item. Then, clutching his key, holding it out, he went back out to the edge for one last look along the curb where stuff might blow up. Augusta came hunching up, saying, Hey, Genevieve, we've got to try that Sony. I said, Keep looking.

Augusta was a horrible sight: hunchbacked, with pocks on her face, an Oklahoma harelip, Lester called it, and lithium teeth, all gone. The soles of her feet had calloused so thick Lester took his razor knife and whittled them out of boredom. Ugly enough to stop a clock, he said when we found her. Ugly enough to stop traffic. Yes, sir, a traffic-stopper indeed, he said, drawing her tight the same way he'd drawn me, making those soft kiss sounds, touching her cheeks, tracing the shape of her face. Oklahoma ugly, he added, lifting up one of her breasts. They're gonna make a movie about this one, he said, taking a step back and boxing his thumbs and fingers to make a frame. Lester had his hopes pinned on being a film director. Post-cleanup, he was going to head to Hollywood. Nothing up in Red Carpet Country can match that for sheer ugliness, he said. I said, You're getting redundant. He said, What? I said, The ugly thing, it's getting old, fast. He said, What did you say? I said, Nothing. He said, I thought so, that's what I thought you said, working a crick out of his neck, twisting it around and around. It was a cold wet October night, somewhere outside Tulsa.

An old farmhouse with a streetlamp attached to the back to ward off prowlers (like us), a huge orb of light casting itself into a mud-rutted backyard filled with whirligigs of all types attached to poles, heaving and rattling in the wind, creating a terrible shudder. Take out that light, Lester said. What? I said.

He said, Get a rock and smash that out. I said, Okay, and went amid the whir of sound to find a rock, picking around for one, looking up at the seesawing figures, the whirling ducks, the swinging shapes. I found a nice round rock and heaved it up at the light and took pleasure in the loud pop and darkness. Get up here, get up here, Lester was yelling from around front. I stood for a minute in the dark and felt the wild ratcheting of the whirligigs in a burst of wind from the west. I knew how they felt. Stuck in eternal toil. I had to save at least one, so I gave a pole a hard kick: a small lumberjack boy in a little green hat, gripping a long saw, looked up at me from the ground and smiled. Get up here, Lester called again from around front. At the front door, working the gray rubber grips of a chrome walker, Augusta's grandfather blinked into the darkness. As soon as he figured out what was going on, he lifted the walker up and used it as a battering ram to hold us back.

When the tape worked lose from his mouth he said, *Augusta, my dear grandchild, you sweet thing.* Augusta just stood with a bewildered look on her face. *Give me a smoke. I need to catch my breath. Give me a cigarette from that pack over there on the counter*, he said. Augusta went over and picked up the long green pack of menthols, shook one out, put it between his lips, found a kitchen match, lit it, and watched while he took a puff, blew and sucked, blew and sucked, blew and sucked until the cigarette fell to the floor. *Put it back*, he said. *Please put it back.*

I'd like to describe her face as otherwise, but truthfully Augusta's eyes in the kitchen that night were flat and mute and silly-looking. They weren't lifeless, exactly, but they were glazed over and sat above her fat cheeks like two raisins pressed into dough while Lester went back into the mudroom, rummaged around, and came out with a broom handle. Give him a whack, he said, holding his fingers up to frame the scene, taking a few steps back, trying as usual to find the right vantage, because from the start, when we met on the train up in Bartlesville, he was making a movie in his head. We were hiding—just two fucked-up kids pulling a ticket scam—in the bathroom, hunched up in there, listening to the conductor whistle as he passed between cars, going through the vapor-seal doors. Lester said something like, My name's Lester and I could make a movie out of your life, leaning low into my face, pressing his beard against my cheek, keeping it there and then moving back, fumbling for a pill and scooping a bit of water from the tiny faucet into his palm—with the pill—and then flopping it expertly into his mouth. You could make a movie of my life? I said. Yeah, he said. I said, Okay. He said, Give me your life. I said, Girl named Genevieve, fucked-up Mom, boyfriend named Vernon, when I slept with Vernon Mom kicked me out of the house, street, street, more of the street, now here. He said, I could do that. I said, Yeah. He said, Okay, I got it, where's all this take place? I said, I'm an Okie girl, all the way, and he said, Hey, me too, that's weird, I'm from Oklahoma, too, the crank state, the old dust bowl state. I said, Okay, that's where we're at. He said, Try this, giving me one of his pills. I said, Okay, taking it while he nuzzled my face, saying, Guys named Vernon are always assholes, for sure. I said, You're right, and we went into one of those high-powered laughing fits, you know, the kind that says we're gonna be together united in love and joy forever, bound by this laugh and this laugh alone. He said, Yeah, I could film your life, leaning down and giving me a kiss, the smell of blue toilet water stinking between us, the coast clear, the train rocking. I said, Where you going and what for? He said, Chicago, to scam tourists on the tour boats. You go on and, like, sit next to them and when they're looking up at the buildings, gawking at the superstructures, you just steal their stuff. I said, That's the plan? He said, It's not much but it works because they're all hayseeds and leave their purses right there, under their chairs, gaping open when they go back to the snack bar to buy cookies and soda. Just reach in and take, take, take, he said, touching my cheek, running his hand while the pills took hold good and tight.

In a movie Augusta would lift her swing over the old man's head and take Lester out with a blow to the temple. Then she'd get me in the brow, or the back of the head. A movie would give you the Bible reading she'd done; you'd get early scenes, in Sunday school, up in the church classroom, smelling of wood wax, of gardenias, Augusta studying the book of Jeremiah, the prophet looking upon Jerusalem, at the wretched state of things, the scorn of the people, saying: *the prophets will become wind, and the word is not in them . . .* Then while the camera panned the whirligigs outside (including the one that I smashed up) a voice would read: *the dead bodies of this people will be food for the birds of the air, and for the beasts of the earth . . .* You'd see her in Sunday school, listening carefully, her face now beautiful and soft, her skin clear, her eyes bright, her hair held back in a ponytail. In the movie you'd see her growing up; you'd see her father trying to get at her; you'd see her own Vernon, Asshole #1, in the flesh. Then you'd see her trying her first, a pale greenie, and

you'd watch as it filled her eyes like a fishbowl. Then she'd untie
her grandfather's wrists and rub them and cry and they'd do a
little square dance of joy, a little do-si-do of happiness. (Because
her grandfather had worked the Muskogee square dance circuit
as Burt Wolverine. He was one of the best.) You'd see them
dancing and then there would be a fade to a scene of him calling
a large dance, people moving in and away from each other,
hooking back, catching, arm in arm, flying out, making kalei-
doscopic formations as they moved.

Lester put his fingers up into a box to make a frame of Augusta
swinging, two-handed, and said, Bingo, that's a take, cut. I said,
Stop. He said, Cut. I said, Stop, Augusta. He said, Cut, cut, and
grabbed her from behind, drawing her up and kissing her head,
saying, That was great, just great, that's a keeper for sure, you
were wonderful, Augusta, you're a brave girl, you're going to
reap awards for that scene alone. Outside, I stood for a moment
in the yard and listened to the soft chatter of the whirligigs
ratcheting, swirling around, sawing and bucking in the wind.
Then I got in the car and sat on the seat next to Lester.

The house went up in a giant wind-fueled blossom that glowed
in the back window of Lester's car while we headed west. I
don't do arson, man, Lester said. Arson is too low on the lad-
der, it's at the bottom of the crime totem pole, for fuck's sake.
That was an act of God, that was something we had nothing to
do with. Even your best arsonist depends too much on the
whims of the elements. What's at the top? I said. He said,
What's at the top? screwing his face up and drawing his fingers

through his beard, pinching it tight. He thought a few minutes. Crucifixion is the top crime, man. No doubt. You nail the palms, you crown the head with thorns, and let slow, natural death take over. The guy up there is high as hell on opiates. Doesn't feel a thing. No, sir. He's blitzed on opiates. No pain, no gain. That's a fact, he said, staring out through the windshield. We were flying swiftly toward the horizon. Darkness was all around us, stretching out across empty plains. The sky was sparkled with stars. Besides us, there wasn't a sign of life in the universe. We were all alone, rattling along at full speed. Just ride the glazed highway to the Holy Land, Lester said. You hang up there on the cross until the birds are pecking your eyes out and then you feel it. When the birds start to peck, the pain begins. When the birds get to your eyes, the opiates cease. Without eyes you're just blessed pain, man, just more and more pain. Lester got quiet for a minute. He reached up one-handed and stroked the tip of his beard. In the dark it was impossible to see his eyes, but I knew what they'd contain if they were visible: he'd have that silence in there, that kind of calm I'd seen before, all dark gray with bits of blue swirled together into the deepest black. When he started talking again, about ten miles later, his voice came out dry and tight. Then all the pain folds up on itself into this vast silky darkness, man, that gets tighter and tighter, tighter and tighter, tighter and tighter, until you're dead, he said. I said, Until you're dead, and tapping the wheel, he said, Yeah, until you're fucking dead. You know how those old TVs used to have that little dot of light when you shut them off? The whole picture would zip into that single little pinpoint of light and then it would sit there, just sitting for a minute, sitting and sitting and then it would zing off to the side and that would be it, you'd be left with just darkness. Well, that's how it is, man.

You bundle it all up, crunch it, and ping, it's gone. He went on about it for a long time that night, nothing more than that memorable to me now, mostly theorizing about why crucifixion is the top crime on the pole, and about what it's like to die, what it's like those final few seconds, just before you sign off, as he said, just before everything becomes static and sizzles out. I said, If it's so top why isn't it done more? He said, Because it's too difficult to find good victims, man. Here in this part of the state it's impossible. Nebraska folk are cleaner, more purified. Tulsa has plenty just waiting for it, man. I said, If they're waiting for it why don't we just go there and find some? He gave this long pause then, rapping the top of the wheel again, adjusting the rearview, looking back at Augusta. You're really a dumb shit, he said. I said, Why? He said, Because Tulsa ones are junkies, and what's dope? Dope's dope, I said. He said, Dope's dopamine, for fuck's sake. You're a Tulsa junkie and you're already there, man. No need to go for the ride because you're on the ride, you see. I said, I see. I didn't, but I said I did. Get up on that cross and you'd like it too much, he said, and then he went into all of the details again, how you'd have to find a couple of pressure-treated railroad ties to make the cross, some of those galvanized nails you use to hang gutters. (Lester had done a lot of roofing in his life and could lay down shingles in his sleep, said thick tar smells remained in his nostrils.) You'd get some high-grade nylon rope. But if you like it too much, I said. What? If you like it too much, I said. What are you talking about? You said if you like it too much, on the cross, you said they'd, the Tulsa guys, would like it too much. He said, So what? So if you like it too much it's not a crime, I said. He said, Yeah, that's it, that's right, exactly, you put some skinny-ass Tulsa junkie up there and he'd go for the ride of his life, but for Augusta you'd have to use a—what's it called?—a block-and-tackle thing, like getting a piano up to an apartment, you know, like that Abbott and Costello routine, he said. I said, What are you talking about? He said, Just thinking about what it would be like to get her up on a cross. We drove. Drove more. By the time we got to Elk City the wind was coming in swoops, nudging us onto the shoulder and then back onto the road. The rage behind it was apparent to us all. You can't go breaking small fragile things without ramifications, I thought, watching Lester grapple with the steering wheel as the wind ground us to a dead stop, hit with such ferocity that the car just couldn't make headway, and we ended wayward on the shoulder, spinning our wheels until Lester eased up and said, Gotta make a pit stop, and opened the door into the roar, crossed in front of the headlights, bending down into the wind, the dust roiling around his head. Out there he was a space walker lost to the world while we sat waiting. I said, Augusta? She said, Yeah? I said, Are you okay? She said, Yeah. I said, You're really beautiful, you know. She said, Yep. I turned and looked: a big mound of flesh topped by a moon face lit by the interior light, her eyes invisible but glassed over, dead to the world because Lester had pumped her full as a reward for her acting skills, for being so brilliant in her role. He'd found the lab in the back shed, a bunch of old bait buckets and chemicals, tubes and glassware, and a huge amount of product. The old coot's a crank cooker, he'd said. You put him in a movie, nobody would believe it. Put him in a movie and they'd bow into their popcorn and mumble: Bullshit, man, he'd said, framing it up with his fingers to see what it might look like.

In a movie I would have ditched Lester right there, snapped the locks, moved over into his seat, and torn out into the night, doing so for my own sake and for Augusta's, saving us both, knowing right from wrong, solving the riddle of our own situation with a single, swift act, turning the tables, finding a foothold on a newfound sense of goodness; he'd be out there in some frozen field, amid the dead husks, taking a piss, when he'd hear the tires squeal, zipping himself up while making one of those funny staggers across the dirt, holding his fingers up into a frame and calling, Cut, cut, cut. In the car we'd give little hoot laughs, girl to girl, and Augusta would speak to me, her voice dry and tight in a Red Carpet tone, and she'd talk in a strange manner, like she was in an old play or something, and she'd say, We've torn ourselves free of the demonic, of the oracle that has given us the word, or something like that in a haunted voice, babbling on and on while I drove all the way to Oklahoma City. We'd get to the memorial in heavy snow. We'd get out of the car and there would be that fake movie night, that night that's not really dark, or light. At least not dark enough to be real. There'd be fake snow on our shoulders, too, sticking to them, refusing to melt, while we went from chair to chair. One chair for each dead person. (I'd sit in one and say something along the lines of: My poor mom died in the blast, gone in a flash, got up one morning and headed for social services unaware that it was her last, and then Augusta, taking her turn, would talk about how her own sister had gone to the day-care center that morning, because her daughter was having problems with separation anxiety, problems parting, saying so long. With the snow coming down—still crying—we'd move from chair to chair, sitting in each one, leaving an impression in the snow on the dark stone. Then the camera would begin to rise above us, up and up, and you'd see the whole scene, chair, snow, girls, night light, the monument to the blast, the empty space, the shadows cast by the chairs, the road leading out, the buildings around it; up and up but always both of us visible, two girls who had somehow rescued themselves from a complete fuckup, from a demented Wind Country guy.) But, you know, the movie ending wouldn't be that simple. Nothing ever is. You'd sit in the theater, scraping the last bits of popcorn from the bucket, knowing that Lester is still out there, probably up in that park, near that rock where the first Oklahoma oil well was sunk, the place that started the whole fucking mess, smoking a joint and racking his brain over where I might be. You'd be aware of this in the theater, as the camera kept moving skyward, and you'd feel a bit of the fear that I felt, then, in the car, knowing that he'd be lodged in your mind, waiting to pop up suddenly, to take advantage of the situation. You'd leave the theater with me in your mind, too, and with Augusta (but a better version of what she really was), and you'd carry me right back to your nice house in Tulsa. You'd drive into your garage, the door closing behind you, and go up the stairs into your warm kitchen for a glass of milk, maybe a cookie, and then to your warm bedroom, with the king-size bed; you'd take me under the covers with you, my eyes, my mouth, my long brown hair, and you'd lie with the blankets up around your chin, safe and sound, and see me inside your mind. I'd be giving you a huge smile, grinning a big, fat, shit-eating grin. Only later, waking to use the bathroom, would you remember Lester. You'd think of him out there, sneaking around, bottled up with a bunch of harebrained schemes, lifting Augusta's breasts. You'd try to shake him out of your mind. But he'd lurk there. Lurking Lester. He'd bug you. Like a tick behind a dog's ear. He'd bug you like the rattle of trucks on an overpass. He'd bug you like the squeal of bats in a cave. Then you'd know how I felt, in the car, when he came back across the headlights, tugging his fly, stopped for a second so that the light carved up under his chin and made his face hollow and skull-like, staring at me, staring hard, as if he knew what I was thinking, and then he slid in next to me, smelling like field mud. I said, What're we gonna do? And he said, We're gonna find a shopping mall, do some receipt hunting, find a way to make some money. Turning around to face Augusta, who had a long silvery strand of drool dripping from the side of her mouth, framing her with his fingers, he said, Then we're going to make us that movie.

The Gulch

The cross was jury-rigged out of pressure-treated wood ties, the kind used for gardening, as borders on raised beds, and for retaining walls, secured at the cross point—for lack of a better term—with a hitch of cotton rope, ashen in color from exposure to the elements, stolen from Mrs. Highsmith's yard; a clothesline that had for several years held the garments of Rudy Highsmith (involved). Fingering it in the evidence room, Detective Collard could feel the droopy sway of a line laden with wet garments, and he could easily imagine Rudy's ragged jeans, holes shredded white, pale blue and growing lighter under the warmth of the sun, picking up the breeze on some late-summer afternoon, while a dog barked rhapsodically along the edge of the woods. The Highsmith house was on the outskirts of Bay City, Michigan, not far from the gulch, and was known—to a few locals, at least—as the house with laundry on the line, one last holdout of the air-drying tradition. The cross was set in a hole that had been dug by a fold-up trench shovel. This was admitted by Ron Bycroff, age seventeen, the oldest in the bunch. Bycroff openly confessed—after five hours of interrogation—to digging the hole and securing the cross and arranging the ropes and so on, but not to the actual pounding of the spikes, nor even to being there at that point. (He was there, he later admitted to his lawyer, but not in spirit and heart, and he had his eyes turned away most of the time. I just couldn't look. I heard the sounds and that was enough.) During the trial, this confession was thrown out by Judge Richards because it had been obtained by coercion. (You'd have to be ashamed, boy, you'd have to be as deeply ashamed as anyone on this good earth, doing what you did, boy. How'd you feel if I took you down there to the gulch myself, right now, to take a little look around? I might just take you down there tonight.) On the other hand, the trench shovel was from the Bycroffs' garage. During his interrogation, Detective Collard was unable to remove from his mind's eye (is there a better phrase?) the impressive vision of the spikes in the victim's palms, deep, dimpling the skin. The small hand, and the blood around the entry point in the beam of his flashlight, had given him a sense of the softness of human flesh and the vulnerability of hands to piercing implements. The skin on the victim's hands—he knew because he reached out and touched one—was soft and smooth, like a chamois, or the inside of a dog's ear.

For his part, Rudy Highsmith laid out the details of the murder between snot-filled snorts, divulging the story in breathy gushes. The whole thing was Al Stanton's idea, he said. He came up with it. Like he was preaching to us. He was saying this weird shit about how it was time to open up the cosmos. He told us Sammy was the perfect age and all, sixteen and a half, and that it would be good for him to rise from the dead. It was all his idea, honest. He came up with it first. This claim, that Stanton was the one who dreamed up the scheme (for lack of a better word), seemed dubious to Detective Collard. The hefty, moonfaced kid—a linebacker on the high school team—seemed dense in thought, a bit slow on the uptake but also openly sweet and likable. His eyes contained a sadness that came—Collard knew—from the fact that his father had disappeared when he was eight, taking off in his bass boat onto Lake Erie. (The most likely scenario was that he drove his boat down to Cleveland, sold it, and headed to Florida to find a new way of life.) His mother, a heavy drinker and prone to violence, showed up every few months on the police blotter as a DWI and eventually became known around the station as a SAWTH, a Serious Accident Waiting to Happen. There were—any policeman could tell you—those who were preordained to fiery deaths, those most certain to be found frozen in a ditch outside of town, those whose future lay out there like a bear trap, ready to snap shut when the right amount of pressure was applied on just the right spot.

Dead faces, Collard thought, often spoke to the world, sending out final messages that were surprisingly heartfelt and concise. Dead lovers wore the betrayed smirks of the heartbroken. Dead adulterers had a worried cast to their mouths. The murdered had the silent look of the betrayed, glancing to one side or the other to indicate the direction of the perpetrator's flight. The tortured held their lips as wide as possible at the arrogance of the living, wanting above all to arrange for a conversation with the future. But the victim of the crime down in the gulch seemed to say something else: his face was resigned and silent and nonassuming. (Collard was fully aware that it was easy to see something that wasn't there, just as some drifter had found the

Virgin Mary in a viaduct in Detroit last winter, recognizing her face in a splotch of salt and snow splatter cast up against the cement pylon by the passing snowplows.)

Collard—who was big on fishing—had a theory that the truth always sat deep, waiting to be snagged and brought to the surface. With the boys in this case, he would later think, his technique had been off. His voice had cracked, his words had arrived unstable. The boy, Stanton, was not exactly cocky. But he was unusually sure-footed and assured when he said that he had nothing to do with the crime, that he had stood to the side while the other kids performed the rites; he had done nothing except pass, at one point, the spikes over to Bycroff, who held them while someone else, maybe Highsmith, maybe not, because he wasn't really looking, pounded them in with the croquet hammer.

Bycroff blamed Stanton, who in turn blamed Highsmith, who went around himself to point his finger at Bycroff in what most detectives traditionally call the golden hoop of blame. This three-way tag of culpability seemed particularly fine to Collard, who had gone so far as to hold the actual gag bandana up in Rudy Highsmith's face during his interrogation. A green, snot-stiff cloth that, when unknotted and straightened, still seemed to hold, in the wavelets of its hardened folds, a residue of the victim's last words.

It was impossible to imagine such agony without inflicting some on yourself, Collard thought, and listening to descriptions

of the event during the trial, he bit his nails to the quick just
to find some small amount of pain from which to extrapolate
the rest. Most in the courtroom did something to this effect.
The jury box was stuffed with nail chewers. Lawyers snapped
their fingers under the clamps of their clipboards; reporters in
the gallery dug their fingers into their arms, pinching hard, as if
to check their consciousness. Most imagined the suffering as a
dreary succumbing to the knowledge of the pain, an almost
delirious unknowing state as the nails came through, the first
bloom of pain, and then a feeling of being fixed there, yielding
to something soft and—at least the way Collard imagined it,
still thinking in terms of the laundry on those lines—fluffy and
smelling of starch. What did it mean, some of the jury won-
dered, to lay claim to the idea that the boy was not suffering
as much as one expected? In an attempt to lighten the immen-
sity of the crime, a pain expert was brought in to testify that
the body did have certain chemicals that came to the defense
of the afflicted in this kind of situation. (Torture, on the
other hand, was a matter of countering the body's natural
opiates, of inducing pain incrementally, with a finesse that
worked around these chemical defenses.) The boys, in their
quick, careless plunge into the heart of whatever it was, darkness or evil (the prosecution couldn't exactly decide), had nailed
the boy to the cross hard and fast, producing a flush of suffering that had produced a flood of endorphins. Shock was nothing but the deepest joke on consciousness, and when this boy,
on that cold fall night, was faced with spikes—through his
hands and legs, as he twisted up against the face of the jury-
rigged cross—he flew the coop, so to speak, and became nothing but a vapor of soul stuff who just so happened to inhabit a
body that was, at that moment, being crucified. (The defense
argued.)

If anyone had to confront the issue at hand it was the coroner, Samuel Kelman, because Bay City seemed to produce a disproportionate number of accidental body piercings: boys fell onto implements, impaled themselves through playful jousting, and were samuraied through the gut with a frequency outside the bounds of normalcy. The coroner took care to avoid an inclination he had to find pleasure in the absurd deaths of those who lay on the slabs for examination. These stunts were generally pulled during the night. Attempts were made to defy physical law. Stupidity was like dust, or the earth itself. He drove home that evening—after the examination of the boy's body, making note of the spike holes, the gash along the mouth, the stress fractures in the wrists; making note of the fact that the boy had died at approximately three in the morning. Driving home, listening to Schubert on the car stereo, he considered the bloodless silence of the boy's open eyes (which he shut), fixed upward, and the paradigmatic (was that the word?) palm holes. The boy's body—slightly glistening, with dimples of fat along the waist—seemed to hold a gentle repose, as if giving in to gravity. (Most of the time a body, during the first hours after death, lifted away from the surface of the table, as if barely tethered. A soul-empty body seemed as light as a seedpod, the brittle shell of a cicada.) Of course, he was seeing what he wanted to see in those eyes, pale and sad, somewhat elegiac, dark gray with a bit of blue around the senseless dilation of the pupils. On the way home—glancing over at the dreary waters of the Saginaw River—his thoughts ranged from puncture wounds to tetanus and then landed naturally upon the one time he had himself been impaled. This was in a town called Branford, near New

Haven, Connecticut, goofing around with his buddies, walking barefoot along a breakwater of cemented boulders, enjoying the sense of being sure-footed against the wind gusts, which were coming hard off Long Island Sound that morning, when he felt something impinge upon his foot. A strange tingling sensation; nothing painful until he looked down and saw the point protruding near his toes. Then he became aware of a numb pain, remote and far off. He began running in panic, the board flopping like a wooden clog while his friends laughed and taunted him until it became clear to them what exactly was going on: He had gone into that realm few kids entered but all thought about. He had stepped on the proverbial nail. (In the car he tried to make sense of the physics of the accident, calculating the amount of force it would take to send a nail all the way through his foot, adding to the formula the fact that he had been stepping hard on the rocks at the time, doing a jaunty balancing act for his friends, until the nail sank in near the forefoot, up far enough to allow it to slide between the metatarsals.) What he could remember more than anything was the odd sense of reorientation the nail had given him, a Polaris of pain, until one kid yanked it out while another held his foot, and he, in turn, unleashed a high seagull scream that sent real gulls sweeping up off the beach and into the sky.

None of the boys attended a church or had any formal religious education. All three devoted their spiritual energies to killing time, going up to the beach to smoke hash, or over to Detroit to smuggle beer across the bridge from Canada, loading it up by the case and transporting it past the lackadaisical border guards. Into the gap these facts formed, folks inserted wedges of philosophical thought and tried to avoid the possibility that the reenactment of a two-thousand-year-old event was pure senselessness on the part of teenagers who in no way meant to crack the universal fabric and urge a messianic event on the world. One commentator on a cable news channel argued that it was important to consider the possibility that these boys, in what was certainly a scattershot approach, were trying to find a way to grace. Good boys from good families had dragged the victim—there was a double-rut line of heel marks from the main road down into the gulch—to the spot under a clear, star-filled, late-fall sky, dug a hole with a fold-up entrenchment tool, and erected a cross, without really thinking. One professor at the University of Michigan made a connection between the trench shovel, the poetry of Wilfred Owen, and the Great War, and argued falsely that the soil in Michigan—glacial gravel in the gulch, with remnants of Lake Erie bed fossils—was close in consistency to the bottom of the trenches at Verdun. Another professor, hearing the story reported on the nightly news, brought forth Walter Benjamin's theory of a messianic cessation of happening. He tried to draw (with shaky logic) a parallel between the mock event, the young ruffians (his words) putting their friend up on the cross, and Benjamin's concept of a "revolutionary chance in the fight for the oppressed past." The deep impulse these kids had was to begin a conversation with the knowable universe and the unknown, hidden part that can be seen only when you rend space-time, he said, throwing his arms wide open before the class and then, composing himself, laying his hands flat on the desk, staying like that for a moment until—as was his habit—he reached up to adjust the dimple of his tie, pulling it tight at his throat. The students, who were used to these sudden outbursts, sat back in their chairs and glanced at one another. They were close in age to the kids in the gulch and found it hard to imagine that these fuckups, probably stoned out of their minds on crystal meth, had anything grand in mind.

For her part, Emma Albee, an English teacher at Bay City High School, felt duty-bound to talk about the event in the gulch. (A team of trauma-control agents had been sent to help those students who were suffering changes in behavior due to the death of their friend—though in truth he had no friends, and was for the most part a loner who had, before his death, secured the wrath of most of his schoolmates.) She spoke carefully to the class, saying, yes, the action of the three boys was evil, in that they were free not to crucify their friend, just as you are free to do something or not to do something. Her students sat, for once, listening with rapt attention. You see, the tragedy of their action, she said, was in the fact that they made a gross error of judgment. We all think about doing things like this, don't we? We all have these strange ideas, and sometimes we're with our friends and we feel pressured to do them, but we do not because we are free, she said, looking for a segue into *The Stranger* by Albert Camus.

Several news accounts made a great deal of the fact that the dead boy's face had been excised from several school yearbooks, cut out neatly with razor blades, removed from the grid. Even Detective Collard had smirked at the kid's image: flyaway hair pasted to a pimply brow; a mouth locked into a grimace, caught off guard by the tired school photographer. (One professor noted a striking resemblance between the victim's face and that of Edgar Allan Poe. The same lean jawbone, the same uncomfortable arrangement between his neck and his lower torso, a general disagreement therein, so that even though he was wearing a striped polo shirt, he still had the bearing of a man in a clerical collar.)

We just felt like doing it, was Bycroff's statement during his confession. We was just trying it out, you know, like maybe he'd rise again and maybe not, but it was worth a shot, because he was such a lightweight in this life. Bycroff had been rejected by a series of foster homes that took him around the state of Michigan, itself the rough shape of a palm. From Kalamazoo to Petoskey, and then in a series of towns on the way back down to Flint, he proved himself deeply incompatible with several domestic situations until at last he found himself under the care of Howard Wood, a surly loner who, most thought, was abusive. We just figured we'd give it a try, the boy said, working his tongue around his teeth, staring up at Collard, who was listening carefully, tapping his notepad with the eraser end of his pencil. He listened and made notes but knew that this boy's confession would be thrown out of court on some technicality. It was a fast-spoken confession. It came too easily to stick. The boy was speaking out of unrelated pains. It was the deeply innocent who often came up with the most honest and realistic confessions of crimes. When they had everything to lose, they often threw themselves into it beautifully, like a cliff diver—or was it a pearl diver? Those native boys who found it within themselves to go into the dark waters, their legs kicking up toward the light, flapping softly, their arms extended as they clutched and grabbed. That was the nature of being a detective in these situations; you had to go as deep as you could with the air in your lungs burning and your arms fully extended in the hope that you might bring a pearl to the surface.

He had faced this dead end before in other cases, the sense that one witness would blame the other and then the other, ad infinitum; the sense that the criminality would be smeared into something impossibly dull, that in the end, when the boys were sentenced and justice was meted out, he would still have questions about the case that would linger for the rest of his life. There was no end to it. He left Bycroff back in the interrogation room, behind the one-way glass, sitting at a wooden table with his chin in his hands. He left him there and went outside to get some sunlight on his face. He stood in the doorway and thought about it. He'd be a retired cop living up north, enjoying the solitude and silence. He'd be fishing on the middle branch of the Au Sable one day, casting a muddler into the stream, enjoying the day, and then he'd think of the gulch case, and it would all come back to him, and he'd remember storming out of the interrogation room into this bright, clear, beautiful light of a fall day in Bay City. He'd cast again into a riffle, thinking about the fish while, at the same time, trying to tweeze apart the facts of the case, remembering the voids, the gaping space between the statements and his failure to get the story straight. He'd spend the rest of the day in the river, or resting on the shore, until his creel was damp and heavy with trout. He'd lift the lid and look in and see the ferns placed around their flanks and their beautiful stripes. Then he'd stand there along the river and feel something else. He was sure of that. By the time he was retired he'd be full of lore, full of the wisdom of a small-town detective who had seen all he could see, acted as witness to the weird manifestations of the human spirit, and he'd have a suspicion that the best way to cope with the darkness of the world was to concentrate on tying flies, on clamping the hook and spinning the feathers taut with silk thread. The incident at the gulch would be the case that stood out from the others; it would be the classic, the one he pulled out of his hat when the conversations were boring, playing gin rummy or bridge; he'd pull the gulch out and present it as an example of how truly dark the times had become; he'd pull it out as an example of the limits of detective work. Every cop had one such case, the true zinger, the one around which the others rotated, and he would remember it clearly, not so much the facts around it, the words, the talk, the boys' attitudes and posturing, their attempts to work around the guilt, but mainly the place itself, silent and gritty, with condoms curled like snakeskins in the weeds, and the ash craters, and the used needles, glinting in the moonlight, and how he went up there by himself over the course of the years, late in the night just before dawn, to shoot his sidearm into the air, taking aim at the cup of the Big Dipper, just plugging away at it like that, not because he was feeling helpless, or that the gulch itself inspired him to fire his gun, but because it was a pleasurable thing to do. He thought about this, standing outside the station house, taking in the sun. Nothing had changed in Bay City since the incident in the gulch. The media came, set up their dishes, sent the story to the world, got it moving around from head to head, and then just as quickly packed up and left it to be forgotten. On the stream at least he'd have the mercy of forgetfulness and the distance of retrospect and time; everything would be faded and somewhat obscure, except for the facts that he remembered, and he'd go back to his casting, he thought out-side the police station, and he'd find mercy in the failings of his memory, and he'd let the case go, feeling his line curling around itself behind him as it swung forward, tapering out the toss of his rod, aligning itself along the point of the tip before unleash-ing smoothly onto the water until the leader, invisible to the fish, guided the fly to a landing at the intended spot. But for now he had to go back in and face the kid named Bycroff and try to get the facts and see who came up with the idea first, who dreamed it up and made it true.

The Actor's House

Passing the actor's house one thought of biker films, of his former edginess, of his beautiful young face on the screen, of his slight lisp—eventually a trademark of sorts—and the way he stood, slightly to one side, and tilted his head, along with the expressiveness of his features, which weren't perfect because there was something wrong in the symmetry of his face, and his nose had been broken and he tended to blink in a way that made you aware of the lens—but that didn't detract from the power of his genius, and he had three Academy Awards to his name. If you knew he lived there (when he did), you saw the house in light of his ownership. Otherwise, it was nothing more than one more grand house along the river in a long line of grand houses, and there was nothing to make it stand apart from all the others except for the wall along the front, which wasn't built by the actor but rather by the next owner, an actress and television talk show host who found the house lacking in security and, two weeks after she moved in, began to modify it—so that, passing it at that time, one thought not only about the actor, but also about the actress, too, because from her modifications one garnered a sense of what she was like: slightly paranoid and a bit antisocial (there was a rumor afloat that some welcome-wagon soul had come to her front door with a pecan pie and had been duly told, in no uncertain terms, to fuck off). So for a few years one passed the house thinking about both souls (the actress and the actor) with a sense that, behind the walls, the actress moved about from room to room fluffing her hair with the flat of her palm, because she had a habit, most knew, of reaching up to touch her hair as if to affirm its existence—beautiful auburn hair that seemed to have as much to do with her fame as anything. But even a few years after the actor was gone, most people thought of him first and then the actress second when they passed the house, hidden behind the wall: high, built of expensive brick, with security devices in the corners on top—small red pinprick beams that couldn't be seen in normal circumstances but could be seen when it was foggy out, or at night from certain angles, coming back from the city. There were security cameras in the trees, too, and tall evergreen bushes planted just inside the wall that grew to shield the upper reaches of the house from view, so that eventually you couldn't see any of the house at all and had to look at the wall and the bushes and imagine the house as it had once been, years ago, before the talk show host/actress and even the actor lived there and the house had been owned by the Grande Dame of the theater who had been, at least in appearance, unconcerned about privacy.

When the actor bought the house there had been a transition period in which those passing it still thought of the Grande Dame first and then the actor second (if at all), and then thought about her roles on Broadway, and in several movies, and

the elegance and almost Gatsbyesque essence of her personal-
ity—the splendid parties she threw over the years on soft
summer nights, with sedans and chauffeurs, bored, smoking,
leaning against fenders, along the curbside. But then, eventually,
over time, thoughts of the Grande Dame faded and the thought
of the actor came first, as the primary owner, and with his ownership a different kind of feeling, when you passed, and a sense
of mystery, because he was an enigmatic actor and known just
as much for his reclusive nature and strange behavior as he was
for the fact that he had grown enormously fat, so that the body
that had once adorned the screen, and before that the stage, was
hidden beneath rings of fat, like a Russian matryoshka doll;
along with the fact that he was known for his ranting and his
bitter anger and the high energy that seemed to reside beneath
his roles in later years when, for example, in one film, he sat
amid the jungle in a Buddha calm and mumbled his lines. Passing in a car, one imagined him shuffling from room to room in
bedroom slippers, muttering to himself, rehearsing new roles
or—in some visions—mumbling old lines that had once given
life to new characters set in stone, so to speak, on the films that
had recorded his gestures. Passing the actor's house one often
thought of a single scene, a favorite, and remembered it while,
at the same time, imagining him fat behind the walls of the
house. Because many knew the house's interior—during those
early days of the actor's ownership—from the tours that had
been given back in the Grande Dame's days, when, once a year,
she had opened her door to the general public and allowed
them to traipse through, fingering the brocade bedspreads and
touching her fine collection of Native American—they'd think
Indian—artifacts, a huge array of drums and cradle boards.
(Go ahead and touch, she liked to say. Touch anything you

want.) Most folks taking the tour did not realize that she had a smaller house downriver, closer to the city, up on the Palisades: a more manageable house in which she spent most of her free time, and that the actor's house, the one that for many years had been attached to her name by the general public, was mainly for show, or to make her feel a certain way. At the big house—nicknamed Wooden Nickel—she felt like the Grande Dame. At the other house—nicknamed Little Penny—she let her hair down and lay casually about and threw small, intimate dinner parties for her friends who came up from the city and admired her humility and the fact that someone so famous could live in such—and these were the words they used— limited circumstances, all the while knowing, of course, that she owned Wooden Nickel, too, along with Little Penny, and that she represented herself to the world—the general public—with Wooden Nickel and felt secure in doing so because she was not only the Grande Dame of Broadway but also a kind soul, altruistic and giving, and had shared the power of her wealth and fame more than most stars. Passing Wooden Nickel, those few who were aware that she owned Little Penny, and that she threw small parties there, were able to imagine both houses and to see the big house, with its widow's walk and stately facade and fantastic backyard—the pool, the guesthouse, the boathouse with the green light—those few were able to see Wooden Nickel in relation to the actress who also owned Little Penny. But even those souls, limited in number, still looked at the house and— if they were in a hurry—thought of her simply and cleanly. Whereas later, after the actor bought the house, if the same souls passed they made a single connection and thought only of him—the actor's house—because as far as anyone knew, it was his only residence. Not only was it his only house, but he lived there alone, too. So it took on the added weight of his isolation. He had moved there, most knew, after the divorce of his third wife, a famous beauty who had starred in a movie with him years earlier, a comedy about mismatched love: a young girl and a much older man who suffered from a form of autism that gave him (in the movie) an innate ability to communicate through his virtuosic piano playing. (And watching that film they couldn't help but remember his old roles and the way, years before, his thick hands, tight in black gloves, had gripped the handlebars of his motorcycle while his hips shifted in his leather pants and his broad shoulders rolled gently beneath his T-shirts.) So passing the actor's house one might think, for no apparent reason, unable to pin down exactly why, about undershirts, and in doing so envision the old actor walking from room to room inside, head bowed, his big gut lurching, moving solemnly, stopping now and then to gaze out the window while he thought about some long-lost moment, a scene from one of his movies, maybe, in which he had embodied some character and given it life only to end up feeling, when the shot was finished, a sense of depletion and loss as he sank down into his chair bereft of whatever creative fuel and psychic juice it had taken to get himself into characters so far from himself—and not even real in the first place—that it seemed impossible, at times, to see across the chasm between the two states: as if he were now nothing but a husk of skin that had once contained those former characters. And it was easy to imagine, passing the house, that he felt empty and depleted all the time now, a remnant not only of his former self but also of his former characters. Eventually, almost everyone in the town who had known the Grande Dame and taken the annual open-house tour of Wooden Nickel forgot most of the details of the interior, with the exception, perhaps, of the cradle boards, and when passing the actor's house they were unable to completely imagine what it was like inside and could only conjure empty rooms defined by walls and the view of the river out the windows: the river, constantly changing, going from placid, glossy smooth one morning—littered with trash and old tree limbs—and then ruffled with long flails of chop the next, always changing and never the same. So they found themselves limited, most of them, to imagining what the actor saw, if he actually looked from his back windows, when he sat alone and gazed out at the water, thinking about his past with a bitter sense of regret over the loss of his third wife, who was dead, or the fact that he had squandered his career under the guise of being a genius, or perhaps because he really was a genius and did not know how to come to terms with the powers that came to him naturally and without study and made him feel uncomfortable: whereas (some passing the actor's house thought) if he had had to train hard and work at the acting, he might've felt a sense of proprietorship over his abilities (and, in turn, the house); whereas, some imagined, passing, he had been helplessly buoyant upon the raging sea of his talents so that, in turn, he could only garner a sense of control over his life by not acting, or by taking bit roles that were far beneath his talents, forcing his so-called genius into small, ill-fitting characters the same way he now squeezed into his ill-fitting clothes.

For a few years the actor's house did the best it could to maintain its former grandeur and to hold on to the Grande Dame for as long as it could until eventually the windows began to warp out of their frames and the eaves sagged, chewed up by carpenter ants, and the paint began to scale along the clapboards. By the time the actor died, one windy fall afternoon, the house was fully his. On the day he died, those passing on the road glanced over and saw the house and perhaps thought: There's the actor's house, and then they thought about his films or looked ahead and simply went on their way, because he had lived there long enough in solitude, without showing his face, to nullify most speculation, and on that brisk fall day the structure had become, quite simply, the actor's house, and not much more.

The Junction

As he heaves down through the weeds with a plate in his hand
and a smear of jelly on his lips we watch him and stay silent.
Our bellies are roaring. Not a full meal in days. Just a can
of beans yesterday—while we wait out the next train—the
Chicago–Detroit most likely, tomorrow around ten—and stay
calm, listening to that high Middle Western bitterness in his
voice as he talks about the pie cherries and the wonderfully
flaky crust and the way he found it steaming on the sill, waiting
for him as he expected. He talks about how the man of the
house was inside listening to a radio show, clearly visible
through the front parlor window, with a shotgun at his side, just
the shadow of it poking up alongside his chair. Same son of a
bitch who chased me out of there a while back, he explains.
Then he pauses for a minute and we fear—I feel this in the way
the other fellows hunch lower, bringing their heels up to the
fire—he'll circle all the way back to the beginning of his story
again, starting with how he had left this camp—a couple of
years back—and hiked several miles to a street, lined with old
maples, that on first impression had seemed very much like the
one he'd grown up on, although he wasn't sure because years of

drifting on the road had worn the details from his memory, so many miles behind him in the form of bad drink and that mind-numbing case of lockjaw he claims he had in Pittsburgh. (The antitoxin, he explained, had been administered just in time, saving him from the worst of it. A kind flophouse doctor named Williams had tended to his wound, cleaning it out and wrapping it nicely, giving him a bottle of muscle pills.) He hiked into town—the first time—to stumble upon a house that held a resemblance to whatever was left in his memory: a farmhouse with weatherworn clapboard. A side garden with rosebushes and, back beyond a fence, a vegetable patch with pole beans. Not just the same house—he had explained—but the same sweet smell emanating from the garden where far back beyond a few willow trees a brook ran, burbling and so on and so forth. He went on too long about the brook and one of the men (who exactly, I can't recall) said, I wish you still had that case of lockjaw. (That was the night he was christened Lockjaw Kid.) He stood out in the road and absorbed the scene and felt an overwhelming sense that he was home; a sense so powerful it held him fast and—in his words—made him fearful that he'd find it too much to his liking if he went up to beg a meal. So he went back down to the camp with an empty belly and decided to leave well enough alone until, months later, coming through these parts again after a stint of work in Chicago (Lockjaw couched his life story in the idea of employment, using it as a tool of sorts to get his point across. Whereas the rest of us had long ago given up talking of labor in any form, unless it was to say something along the lines of: Worked myself so hard I'll never work again; or, I'd work if I could find a suitable form of employment that didn't involve work) he decided to hike the six miles into town to take another look, not sure what he was searching for because by that time the initial visit—he said last time he told the story—had become only a vague memory, burned away by drink and travel; aforesaid confession itself attesting to a hole in his story about having worked in Chicago and giving away the fact that he had, more likely, hung on and headed all the way out to the coast for the winter, whiling his time in the warmth, plucking the proverbial fruit directly from the trees and so on and so forth. We didn't give a shit. That part of his story had simply given us a chance to give him a hard time, saying, You were out in California if you were anywhere, you dumb shit. Not anywhere near Chicago looking for work. You couldn't handle Chicago winters. Only work you would've found in Chicago would've been meat work. You couldn't handle meat work. You're not strong enough to lug meat. Meat would do you in, and so on and so forth. Whatever the case, he said, shrugging us off, going on to explain how he hiked the six miles up to town again and came to the strangely familiar house again: smell of the brook. (You smelled the brook the first time you went up poking around, you dumb moron, Lefty said. And he said, Let me qualify and say not just the smell but the exact way it came from—well, how shall I put this? The smell of clear, clean brook water—potable as all hell—filtered through wild myrtle and jimsonweed and the like came to me from a precise point in my past, some exact place, so to speak.) He stood outside the house again, gathering his courage for a knock at the back door, preparing a story for the lady who would appear, most likely in an apron, looking down with wary eyes at one more vagrant coming through to beg a meal. I had a whopper ready, he said, and then he paused to let us ponder our own boilerplate beg-tales of woe. Haven't eaten in a week & will work for food was the basic boilerplate, with maybe the following flourish: I suffered cancer of the blood (bone, liver, stomach, take your pick) and survived and have been looking for orchard work (blueberry, apple) but it's the off-season so I'm hungry, ma'am. That sort of thing. Of course his version included lockjaw. Hello, ma'am, I'm sorry to bother you but I'm looking for a meal & some work. (Again, always the meal & work formula. That was the covenant that had to be sealed because most surely the man of the house would show up, expecting as much.) He moved his mouth strangely and tightened his jaw. I suffered from a case of lockjaw back in Pittsburgh, he told the lady. I lost my mill job on account of it, he added. Then he drove home the particulars—he assured us—going into not only Pittsburgh itself (all that heavy industry), but also saying he had worked at Homestead, pouring hot steel, and then even deeper (maybe this was later, at the table with the entire family, he added quickly, sensing our disbelief) to explain that once a blast furnace was cooked up, it ran for months and you couldn't stop to think because the work was so hard and relentless, pouring ladles and so on and so forth. Then he gave her one or two genuine tears, because if Lockjaw had one talent it was the ability to cry on command. (He would say: I'm going to cry for you, boys, and then, one at a time, thick tears would dangle on the edges of his eyelids, hang there, and roll slowly down his cheeks. Oft times he'd just come back to the fire, sit, rub his hands together, and start the tears. You'll rust up tight, Lockjaw, one of the men would inevitably say.) In any case, the lady of the house—she was young with a breadbasket face, all cheek bones and delicate eyes—looked down at him (he stayed two steps down. Another technique: always look as short and stubby and nonthreatening as possible) and saw the tears and beckoned him with a gentle wave of her hand, bringing him into the kitchen, which was warm with the smell of baking bread. (Jesus, our stomachs twitched when he told this part. To think of it. The warmth of the stove and the smell of the baking! We were chewing stones! That's how hungry we were. Bark & weeds.) So there he was in the kitchen, watching the lady as she opened the stove and leaned over to poke a toothpick into a cake, pulling it out and holding it up, looking at it the way you'd examine a gemstone while all the time keeping an eye on him, nodding softly as he described—again—the way it felt to lose what you thought of as permanent employment after learning all the ropes, becoming one of the best steel pourers—not sure what the lingo was, but making it up nicely—able to pour from a ladle to a dipper to a thimble. (He'd gotten those terms from his old man. They were called thimbles, much to the amusement of the outside world. His father had done millwork in Pittsburgh. Came home stinking of taconite. He spoke of his father the way we all spoke of our old men, casually, zeroing in as much as possible on particular faults—hard drinking, a heavy hand. The old man hit like a heavyweight, quick and hard, his fist out of the blue. The old man had one up on Dempsey. You'd turn around to a fist in your face. A big ham-fisted old brute bastard. Worked like a mule and came home to the bottle. That sort of thing.) In any case, he popped a few more tears for the lady and accepted her offer of a cup of tea. At this point, he stared at the campfire and licked his lips and said, I knew the place, you see. The kitchen had a familiar feel, what with the same rooster clock over the stove that I remembered as a boy, you see. Then he tapered off again into silence and we knew he was digging for details. Any case, no matter, he said. At that point I was busy laying out my story, pleading my case. (We understood that if he had let up talking he might have opened up a place for speculation on the part of the homeowner. The lady of the house might—if you stopped talking, or said something off the mark—turn away and begin thinking in a general way about hoboes: the scum of the world, leaving behind civility not because of some personal anguish but rather out of a desire—*wanderlust* would be the word that came to her mind—to let one minute simply vanish behind another. You had to spin out a yarn and keep spinning until the food was in your belly and you were out the door. The story had to be just right and had to begin at your point of origin, building honestly out of a few facts of your life, maybe not the place of birth exactly but somewhere you knew so well you could draw details in a persuasive, natural way. You drew *not* from your own down-and-out-of-luck story, because your own down-and-out-of-luck story would only sound sad-sack and tawdry, but rather from an amalgamation of other tales you'd heard: a girlfriend who'd gone sour, a bad turn of luck in the grain market, a gambling debt to a Chicago bootlegger. Then you had to weave your needs into your story carefully, placing them in the proper perspective to the bad luck so that it would seem frank & honest & clean-hearted. Too much of one thing—the desire to eat a certain dish, say, goulash, or a hankering for a specific vegetable, say, lima beans—and your words would sound tainted and you'd be reduced to what you really were: a man with no exact destination trying to dupe a woman into thinking you had some kind of forward vision. A man with no plans whatsoever trying as best he could—at that particular moment—to sound like a man who knew, at least to some degree, where he might be heading in relation to his point of origin. To speak with too much honesty would be to expose a frank, scary nakedness that would send the lady of the house off—using some lame excuse to leave the room—to phone the sheriff. To earn her trust, you sat there in the kitchen and went at it and struck the right balance, turning, as a last resort, to the facts of railroad life, naming a particular junction, the way an interlocking mechanism worked, or how to read semaphores, for example, before swinging back wide to the general nature of your suffering.) We knew all of the above and even knew, too, that when he described, a moment later, the strange all-knowing sensation he got sitting in that kitchen, that he was telling us the truth, because each of us had at one point or another seen some resemblance of home in the structure of a house, or a water silo, or a water pump handle, or the smell of juniper bushes in combination with brook water, or the way plaster flaked, up near the ceiling, from the lath. Even men reared in orphanages had wandered upon a particular part of their past. All of us had stood on some lonely street—nothing but summer afternoon chaff in the air, the crickets murmuring drily off in the brush— and stared at the windows of a house to see a little boy staring back, parting the curtain with his tiny fingers.

You sit down to the table, set with the good silver, the warmth of domestic life all around, maybe a kid—most likely wide-eyed, expecting a story of adventure, looking you up and down without judgment, maybe even admiration, while you dig in and speak through the food, telling a few stories to keep the conversation on an even keel. You talk about train junctions, being as specific as possible, making mention of the big one in Hammond, Indiana, the interlocking rods stretching delicately from the tower to the switches. Then you use that location to spin the boilerplate story about the sick old coot who somehow traveled from Pittsburgh or Denver (take your pick), making a long journey, only to find himself stumbling and falling across one of the control rods, bending it down, saving the day because the distracted and lonely switchman up in the tower had put his hand on the wrong lever (one of those stiff Armstrong levers) only to find it jammed up somehow—ice froze, most likely, because the story was usually set at dawn, midwinter—and then had sent a runner kid out to inspect the rod, and when the runner kid was out the switchman had gone to the board and spotted his error, and the runner kid (you slow down and key in to this point) found the half-dead hobo lying across the rod. You shift to the runner's point of view. You explain how during the kid's year on the job he had found a dozen or more such souls in the wee hours of dawn: young boys curled fetal in the weeds; old hoboes, gaunt and stately, staring up at the sky; men quivering from head to toe while their lips uttered inane statements to some unseen partner. You shake your head and mention God's will, fate, Providence, luck, as the idea settles across the table—hopefully, if you spun the yarn correctly—that hoboes do indeed serve a function in God's universe. (Not believing it one whit, yourself.) If the point isn't taken, you backtrack again to the fact that if the switchman had pulled the lever, two trains would've collided at top speed coming in, each one, along the lovely, well-maintained—graded with sparkling clean ballast to keep the weeds down—straightaway, baked up good and hot for the final approach, eager, wanting in that strange way to go as fast as possible before the inevitable slowdown—noting here that nothing bothers an engineer more than having to brake down for a switch array, hating the clumsy, awkward way the train rattles from one track to another. To spice it up, if the point still hasn't been taken, you fill them in on crash lore, the hotbox burnouts—overheated wheel journal accidents of yore; crown sheet failures—a swhooooosh of superheated steam producing massive disembowelments, mounds of superheater tubes bursting out of the belly of enormous engines, spilling out like so much spaghetti. All of those unbelievable catastrophic betrayals of industrial structure that result in absurd scenes: one locomotive resting atop another, rocking gently while the rescue workers, standing to the side, strike a pose for the postcard photographer. You go on to explain the different attitudes: engineers who dread head-ons, staring mutely out into the darkness while the brakeman grabs his flagging kit—fuses, track torpedoes—and runs ahead to protect the train.

At the dining room table with the entire family, Lockjaw had turned to the boilerplate story, personalizing it by adding that he had been given medical care in Pittsburgh (an injection of antitoxin by a kindly charity doctor; the wound cleaned out and bandaged; a bottle of muscle pills to boot) and found himself wandering off before the cure set in, only to collapse several hundred miles away on the rods at Stateline junction, giving all the details—about the rods, the way the tower worked—and keeping the tone even and believable until the entire table was wide-eyed for a moment, with the exception of the man of the house who, it turned out, had done a stint as a brakeman on the Nickleplate, worked his way up to conductor, and then used his earnings to put himself through the University of Chicago Law School. The man of the house began asking questions, casually at first, not in a lawyerly voice but in a fatherly tone, one after another, each one more specific, until he had a lawyerly tone that said, unspoken: Once you've eaten you pack yourself up and ship out of town before I call the sheriff on you. Go back to your wanderlust and stop taking advantage of hardworking folks. Right then, Lockjaw thought he was safe and sound. Dinner & the boot. Cast off with a full belly, as simple as that. But the lawyerly voice continued—Lockjaw went into this in great detail, spelling out how it had shifted from leisurely cross-examination questions—You sure you fell across a rod hard enough to bend it? You sure now you saved the day exactly as you're saying, son? To tighter, more exact questions: Where you say you're from? What kind of work you say you did in Pittsburgh? Did you say you poured from a ladle into a thimble, or from a ladle into a scoop? You said interlocking mechanism? You sure those things aren't fail-safe? You said an eastbound and a westbound approach on the same line? (At this point, most of the men around the fire knew how the story would turn. They understood the way in which such questions pushed a man into a corner. Each answer nudged against the last. Each answer depended on a casualness, an ease and quickness of response, that began to give way to a tension in the air until the man of the house felt his suspicions confirmed in the way the answers came between bites, because you'd be eating in haste, making sure your belly was as full up as fast as possible, chewing and turning to the lady, and, as a last ditch, making mention of a beloved mother who cooked food almost, but not quite, nearly, but not exactly, as good. These are the best biscuits I've ever had, and that's factoring in the fact that I'm so hungry. Even if I wasn't this hungry, I'd find these the best biscuits I've had in my entire life.)

When Lockjaw told this part of the story, the men by the fire nodded with appreciation because he was spinning it all out nicely, building it up, playing it out as much as he could, heading toward the inevitable chase-off. One way or another the man of the house would cast him off his property. He'd stiffen and adjust his shirt collar, clearing his throat, taking his time, finding the proper primness. A stance had to be found in which casting off the hobo would appear—to the lady of the house— to be not an act of unkindness but one of justice. Otherwise he'd have an evening of bitterness. When the man turned to God—as expected—after the cross-examination about work, employment, and the train incident—Lockjaw felt his full belly pushing against his shirt—a man could eat only so much on such a hungry gut, of course—and had the cup to his mouth when the question was broached, in general terms, about his relationship to Christ. Have you taken Christ? the man said, holding his hands down beside his plate. Have you taken Christ as your Holy Savior and Redeemer? (I knew it. Fuck, I knew it, the men around the fire muttered. Could've set a clock to know that was coming. Can't go nowhere without being asked that one.) At that point, the man of the house listened keenly, not so much to the answer—because he'd never expect to get anything but a yes from a hobo wanting grub—but to the quickness of the response, the pace with which Lockjaw had said, Yes, sir, I took Christ back in Hammond, Indiana, without pausing one minute to consider the width and breadth of his beloved Lord, as would a normal God-fearing soul, saved by Christ but still unable to believe his good grace and luck. (Gotta pause and make like you're thinking it out, Lefty muttered. Gotta let them see you think. If they don't see you thinking, you ain't thinking.) Lockjaw had given his answer just a fraction of a second too quickly, and in doing so had given his host a chance to recognize—in that lack of space between the proposed question and the given answer—the flimsiness of his belief. Here Lock-jaw petered off a bit, lost track of his train of thought, and slugged good and hard from the bottle in his hand, lifting it high, tossing his head back and then popping the neck from his lips and shaking his head hard while looking off into the trees as if he'd find out there, in the dark weeds, a man in white robes with a kind face and a bearded chin with his arms raised in blessing. Fuck, he said. All the man of the house saw was a god-damn hungry tramp trying to scare up some grub. We faced off while his wife prattled away about the weather, or some sort of thing, giving her husband a look that said: Be nice, don't throw him out until he's had a slice of my pie. But the man of the house ignored her and kept his eyes on mine until he could see right into them, Lockjaw said, pausing to stare harder into the woods and to give us time enough to consider—as we warmed our feet—that it was all a part of the boilerplate: The man of the house's gaze would be long & sad & deep & lonely & full of the anguish of his position in the world, upstanding & fine & good & dandy & dusted off, no matter what he did for a liv-ing, farming or ranching or foreclosing on farms, doctoring or lawyering—no matter how much dust he had on him during his work he'd be clean & spiffy with a starched collar & watch chain & cufflinks & lean, smooth, small fingers no good for anything, really, except sorting through papers or pulling a trig-ger when the time came. A little dainty trigger finger itching to use an old Winchester tucked upstairs under the bed, hazy with lint but with a bullet in the chamber ready for such a moment: cocky young hobo comes in to beg a meal and wins over the lit-tle wife only to sit at the table with utter disrespect, offering up cockamamie stories that make the son go wide-eyed and turn the heart.

As Lockjaw described the stare-down with the man of the house, his voice became softer, and he said, The man of the house excused himself for a moment. He begged my pardon and went clomping up the stairs, and I told the lady I probably should be going but she told me about her pie, said she wanted me to have a bite of it before I left, and I told her maybe I'd have to pass on the pie, and we went together to the kitchen, he said while we leaned in intently and listened to him because the story had taken a turn we hadn't expected. For the sake of decorum, most of us would've stayed at the table until the gun appeared. Most of us would've stuck it out and held our own as long as we could, sensing how far we might push it so that the lady would at least give him—the man of the house—a piece of her mind, saying, Honey, you're being hard on the poor boy. He doesn't mean any harm. Put that gun away. Even if his story was a bit far-fetched, he's just hungry, and so on and so forth, while the cold, steely eyes of the man of the house bore the kind of furtive, secretive message that could only be passed between a wandering man, a man of the road, and a man nailed to the cross of his domestic life.

Months ago, when he first told the story, Lockjaw had explained that he'd gone off into the kitchen with the lady (while overhead the man of the house clomped, dragging the gun out from under the bed), who gave a delightful turn, letting her hair, golden and shiny and freshly washed, sway around her head, leaning down lightly to expose her delicate, fine neck, and then leaning a bit more so that her skirt pressed against the table while she cut him a slice of pie. Right then I felt it and knew it and was sure of it, he said. I was sure that she was my mother and had somehow forgotten me, or lost whatever she had of her ability to recognize me. I know it sounds strange, he added, pausing to look at us, going from one man to the next, waiting for one of us to make a snide remark. The rooster clock in the kitchen and the layout and the fact that the street was exactly like the one I grew up on and the way the pump handle outside the kitchen window was off balance; not to mention the willows out back, and beyond them that smell of the creek I mentioned, and the way the barn had been converted to serve as a garage for the car, and the fact that around the time I took to the road my mother was readying to have another son, and that boy would've been close to the right age by my calculation— give or take—to be the one she wanted. I would've asked her to confirm my premonition if the old man hadn't come down and chased me clean out of there before I could even have a bite.

Whatever the case, Lockjaw had fooled himself into believing his own story, one way or another, and across the fire that night he had dared us to put up some bit of sense in the form of a question, just one, but none of us had it in him to do so because we were too hungry. (At least I think this is why we let him simply close his story down. He shut it down and began to weep. He cried in a sniffy, real sort of way, gasping for breath, cinching his face up tight into his open palms, rubbing them up into his grief again and again. He was faking it, Hank said later. He was pulling out his usual trump card. He had me up until that point. Then his story fell apart.) None of us said a word as night closed over us and the fire went dead and we slept as much as we could, waking to stare up into the cold, flinty sky, pondering the meal he had eaten—the green beans waxy and steaming, the mashed potatoes dripping fresh butter, and of course the pork, thick and dripping with juice, waiting to be cut into and lifted to the mouth of our dreams. Then the train came the next day and we went off into another round of wander—west through Gary, through the yards, holding on, not getting off, sticking together for the most part, heading to the coast for the winter and then east again until we found ourselves at the same junction a year later, the same trees and double switch and cross-tracks where the line came down out of Michigan and linked up with the Chicago track, and once again, as if for the first time, Lockjaw said he recognized the place and then, slowly, bit by bit, he remembered the last visit and said he was going back, heading up through the verge with his thumbs hooked in his pockets, turning once to say he'd try to bring us back a bit of pie. By golly, she said she'd put the pie on the sill for me, he said. She told me anytime I wanted to come back, she'd have it waiting for me. If you remember what I told you, I was running out the door with the gun behind me when she called it out to me, he added, turning one last time before he disappeared from sight. (Forgot all about that foolishness, Hank said. Guess he's home again, Lefty said. And we all had a big, overripe belly laugh at the kid's expense, going on for a few minutes with the jibes, because in Lincoln and in Carson and Mill City and from one shitting crop town to the next he had come back from whatever meal he had scrounged up with the same kind of feeling. He seemed to have an instinct for finding a lady willing to give in to his stories.) By the time he came back the jokes were dead and our hunger was acute. Like I said before, he had the pie on his face and a plate in his hand and he's already talking, speaking through the crumbs and directly to our hunger, starting in on it again, and when he comes to the smell of the brook, we interrupt only to make sure he doesn't go back over the story from the beginning again, sparking him with occasional barbs, holding back the snide comments but in doing so knowing—in that heart of hearts—that we'll make up for our kindness by leaving him behind the next morning, letting him sleep the sleep of the pie, just a snoring mound up in the weeds.